nice boy

a novel by
george veltri

city lights books
san francisco

10 9 8 7 6 5 4 3 2 1

This is a work of fiction. Names, characters, places and incidents are either the product of the author's imagination or are used fictitiously. Any resemblance to actual events, locales, or persons living or dead, is entirely coincidental. All conversations among the characters and their actions are imagined.

Cover design by Rex Ray
Book design by Althea St. Amand
Typography by Harvest Graphics

Library of Congress Cataloging-in-Publication Data

Veltri, George.
      Nice boy : a novel / by George Veltri.
            p.   cm.
      ISBN 0–87286–302–6 (paperback)
      I. Title.
PS3572.E43N53   1995
813'.54—dc20   95–9776
                                                        CIP

City Lights Books are available to bookstores through our primary distributor: Subterranean Company. P. O. Box 160, 265 S. 5th St., Monroe, OR 97456. 503-847-5274. Toll-free orders 800-274-7826. FAX 503-847-6018. Our books are also available through library jobbers and regional distributors. For personal orders and catalogs, please write to City Lights Books, 261 Columbus Avenue, San Francisco CA 94133.

CITY LIGHTS BOOKS are edited by Lawrence Ferlinghetti and Nancy J. Peters and published at the City Lights Bookstore, 261 Columbus Avenue, San Francisco, CA 94133.

Acknowledgments

Thanks to my parents who tried to teach me unselfishness. It didn't work, although I admire them immensely for it. Thanks to my brother for bringing Ahmad Jamal into the house. To my sister for loving me. In memory of Alice and Louise who convinced me for absolute certain that all dogs are good. Thanks to Hannalore Hahn who showed me how it's all poetry. Thanks to Charlotte Walker, a writer and teacher, who embraced my story and me. Thanks to Sheila Beemer, a potter, who told me about trusting my instincts. Thanks to Caroline June and Heidi Bowne who gave me the living room. To Stepka who played chess with me and suffers more than I do. Thanks to Kathryn Kurtz who said, "it's important." To Bill Corsa who did not give up, who constantly sent me messages telling me that what I was doing was good (and he should know). To Bill's partner, Peter Sherred, who believed till the day he died. To Marta Nichols who teaches me how to be joyous, and sad. To Althea St. Amand, the perfect editor for me, and Nancy J. Peters, the perfect publisher, who have not asked me (not even hinted) to be other than who I am.

This book is dedicated to those who struggle in vain against suffering.

Contents

Dead-Phily

There was two Philys in the neighborhood.

One was Phily Murphy. The other was Dead-Phily.

Nobody liked Phily Murphy too much. He hung himself in jail because some men there tough him up. But everybody liked Dead-Phily.

Dead-Phily got one of those moon faces, round-like. And he moved like the moon, not too fast. "So's I don't knock nobody over," he says. Then his moon grin says, "an so's I don't knock me over too."

Dead-Phily's voice slowly dying, maybe that's why he talks so slow, saving what he got left. Could hardly hear it sometimes when he got dope in him. Just a dark hissy whisper then.

Once me and Dead-Phily go to the connection's house together. Was some part of winter. We get inside and wait, sitting on a raggy old couch with paint chips from the ceiling and cockroaches from everywhere. Not like my house.

We're wet. Slush on our feet. Dead-Phily got on cheap sneakers. I got some sort of boot on. My boots are all melting in the house. Makes a little puddle by my feet on the dirty wooden floor. I notice this while Phily's talking, real low, to the connection.

Phily's saying, "what you got, Rose?" Rose, the connection, a deep, deep, brown lady with skin so tight on her face it looks like she might split open any time if she changes her expression at all. Which she don't.

Rose says, "got deuces and dime bags, looking good. Just come in the other day, honey." She calls Phily, honey, but don't smile doing it. We do the deal.

Then Dead-Phily asks Rose, "Rose you mind we do it up here?"

Rose says, "naw, but it'll cost you a bag." I look at Phily. He's already tugging one bag free from the bundle. One small bag, size like maybe if you fold a matchbook in three. Rose ties up ten in a bunch like that with rubber bands.

"You got any gimmicks?" says Rose.

"My traveling companions," says Phily, and he holds up an eyedropper with a baby pacifier stuck on one end. Then he fishes in his pocket and comes up with a needle. "Gimme a dollar," he says to me.

"I got it," I say, and tear a thin strip off the dollar, the little white border along the edge. I hand it to Phily. Phily licks the strip wet and wraps it around the thin end of the eyedropper and snugs the plug end of the needle over it. Wiggles it till it's tight. Nice. The other end with the pacifier works like a syringe pump, squeeze it and let it go for suction. We smile. I notice Dead-Phily's teeth look rotten.

Dead-Phily gets off first since he's sicker than me. He's all the time sicker than me. Phily been shooting dope longer and got himself an ugly habit which keeps him sick most of the time. He don't get up to take off his belt, just lifts up his behind enough to tug, slide it off.

"Match?" I hear him say. I don't catch all of what he says, but that don't matter. Then he says, "Rose, you got a cooker?"

Rose's cooker is just a screw cap from some cheap bottle of wine. Rose's got a bobby pin spread around it so it works like a handle. Tiny handle. Tiny cooker.

Got an old piece of cotton still in it, smushed into the rim

2

from the last junkie who used it. Supposed to be a filter but it's been used a lot and packed down tight now from squeezing it dry, and got a lot of heroin dirt all in it. But that's what makes it good to keep, too. Probably always be in there, till somebody so sick they eat it! Dumb thing to do.

Dead-Phily cooks up the dope, his hand steady with a paper match under the black tin cap. The heroin powder melts in the tiny squirt of water he mixed. Dead-Phily draws up the dope in the eyedropper by squeezing the baby pacifier and letting it go.

He's got the dropper in his teeth now, sideways like a pirate knife. He's doing this so he's got a free hand to pull his belt tight, wrapped around his arm for a tourniquet. He's got the belt on the low part of his arm, Dead-Phily uses the veins on the back of his hand, his pit vein so beat and wore out. After it's tight he holds the loose end of the belt between his knees and reaches for the dropper like some cross-eyed doctor. Even with the belt tied tight, Dead-Phily's nearly dead veins hardly pop up at all. Dead-Phily don't tap-tap the needle in, he digs it in. Like using a screwdriver to pry up some nails. And I'm thinking, the right tool for the right job. He digs it this way and that and finally pins the wiggly string vein, and sticks it.

Dead-Phily's sweating. Blood comes up in the dropper and mixes with the dope. Phily squeezes the pacifier and the blood and dope mix goes down the dropper, into the vein. Dead-Phily's not smiling yet. He lets go of the pacifier and blood comes back up again. And he squeezes it back down again. Now Dead-Phily's smiling. That sleepy, moon smile. Phily's teeth don't look rotten no more.

I say, "come on, you done?" Dead-Phily's just sitting there, the needle and the dropper hanging from his arm. Blood starts seeping up a third time but Phily don't care no more. I reach over, squeeze it back down, and slide the needle out of Phily's arm. My turn, Dead-Phily's done.

I'm all of a sudden sicker than I was. Got anxious and nervous falling all over me. I break open two bags. Takes forever. I use a small glass of water Rose got sitting on the side of the old couch to swish Dead-Phily's blood out of the dropper. I suck up some not so sparkly clean water and squirt it in the cooker. Tiny hairpin handle's hard to hold. My hand's shaking. Heating up the cooker, I burn my finger.

"Oh shit." The cooker falls in the puddle by my feet. I don't think about nothing. Pop off the needle, use the dropper to suck up what I can off the floor. Brown pieces of this and that floating around. "Lost some but got some too," I say, but nobody's listening.

I jam the needle back on. Take Dead-Phily's belt off Dead-Phily's arm. Phily ain't smiling now. Phily's not nothing now. Belt goes on my arm. Pull tight. Hold the loose end in my teeth. Big hungry vein comes up right away. Holding the dropper like a dart, thumb and two fingers. Easy stab, easy stab. I play with the blood, like Phily, two or three times, idea being like shaking up water in an almost empty ketchup bottle, to get what's left. Only my blood's brown, not lipstick color, like Phily's. Mine's got mud puddle in it. Not sick anymore. Sweating stopped. Shaking stopped. Everything is warm.

A light buzz conversation coming from somewhere. Reminds me of them buzz things you hear in summer trees. Starts out low then winds up high, then stops. Usually means it's hot. Usually August. Usually backyard. In one of the fruit trees.

I think I say, "good dope," to Phily, but feel like slowly hardening lead. I'm looking at Dead-Phily. He looks like a dumpling. Phily went from sick, to warm, to happy, to blob. More buzzy voices. I'm looking at Dead-Phily, still.

Dead-Phily's sliding off the couch. Dead-Phily's sliding toward the door. I see Dead-Phily's hand dragging in my dope puddle.

"Your hand's getting wet, Phily," I think I say.

Phily's being dragged to the door. Some clumsy bumping

4

with the door. Old door. Paint falling off that too. Chips falling on Dead-Phily's face.

"Your face, Phily — ." But I realize his eyes are closed, so I don't worry.

Dead-Phily heave-ho out the door. Sunlight comes in. Rose is holding the door open. Somebody else got Phily by the armpit, pulling him across cracks in the sidewalk. Dead-Phily's face is still moon-like, sleeping though. Dump Dead-Phily in the gutter. I'm still sitting on the couch. Dope increased the gravity in me beyond any ability to move.

The sunlight and the buzz sounds make me dream. And I remember a time when me and Dead-Phily was on the Atlantic Avenue bus. Smelly old bus. We were good and high, and had more dope to get high later on. And Dead-Phily was saying to me as the bus went through the Crescent Street overpass, "You make it three winters shooting dope and you're a dope fiend for sure." He grinned his rotten teeth like they was moon rocks.

And the light was shining behind Phily as we come out of the tunnel. He was sitting by the window. I looked past him at the buildings going by. I remember live Phily telling me then, it's like a club to join, junkie club, but watch out. Dead-Phily said it better.

How'd I get home? How'd I get off Rose's crumbling old couch, with all that Palmetto Street dead dope in me? Don't know.

Back in the neighborhood, at the local park, people saying, "Hey, where's Dead-Phily?"

"I dunno," is what I said. "Ain't he here?"

Next day cops find Dead-Phily in a dead gutter. Dead.

Douglas and Me

I get it all figured out. Easy. Go away for the weekend. Away from the neighborhood, away from the dope. Be a moving man, make some legal bucks.

Aqueduct, Belmont, Saratoga racetracks got to move their equipment all around, everything but the horse. And McDunn told my brother-in-law they'd be needing some extras. I'm gonna do that.

I also got it I'm gonna kick some stupid heroin. Some stupid heroin. I look at my arm. Supposed to be looking like ready for hard work. Like mom and dad, and aunt and uncle hard work. But it don't look like that, it looks like dope junkie drug work.

I remember Dead-Phily telling me, "you know them veins only as good as some rubber tire. Patch it up, patch it up. Sooner or later it don't take a patch." He showed me his left arm, all dotted, blue and green-like. "Then you switch to the other arm," he said, "then your fingers and then your toes. Some girls use below their belly. Guys I know go for the jugular. Big, fat, purple worm-like," he says to me, grinning his rotten teeth. His rotten teeth was the first to go far as I remember.

So I'm going to be a moving man. Lift computers and heavy weight horseshit. Nice to be up in the country though. Saratoga. Lots of big men on the job and this boy's gonna be a big man. And I lift and I roll and I shove with what I got.

Not much. I'm feeling so hollow. How'd I lift anything? How'd I lift me?

Not many men talk to me on the move job, but it don't matter. Time we unload in Saratoga, I'm sick. I'm kicking. Dumb word, kicking. Kicking seems like old talk. Like people who don't know nothing about it talk. But kicking's what you do. You kick at nothing. It's stupid, kicking on a racetrack, moving, with moving men. To get my ninety dollars. To get my dope. No sense lying to myself. Been lying enough. Money from this job's going straight in my arm.

Soon as I get back I roust up Douglas. Douglas lives with his mom on 106th Street, the other side of Atlantic Avenue. Douglas got that blond-hair, beach-boy look. All the time smiling. All the time good-looking.

Douglas and me we split up knives. We grab what loose change his mom got laying around. And we get to Brownsville. Brooklyn. Was like the middle of the afternoon. We're all set. Not afraid of the neighborhood, I got "moving man" in me now. Douglas'll learn from me.

We get up to Gladys'. And Ran-dell is there. I do all that communication stuff. Me and Douglas, we get sixteen bags for what we got.

"Thanks, Gladys."

"Later, Ran-dell."

On the way down the block, Palmetto Street, three boys, maybe fourteen, fifteen years old, one breaks a bottle in my back. Breaks the skin. I can feel it break. Douglas got two elbows hooked all over his face.

They're taking our knives! "Motherfuck."

I look at Douglas. He looks so white, and so, boy. Not like the moving men. So we give up the dope. Our dope. My racetrack dope. Douglas' mama's card money dope. Now we got no dope. And we got no knives.

And the mugger boys singing, "Now git!"

Three old ladies in their rocking chairs across the street watching us. We git. Oh shit, we git. We're so past sad, I cry.

Douglas says, "Men don't cry."

Zazz

I got black hair. Brown, and sometimes green, eyes. Depends on the time of day. Girls tell me I got long eyelashes and this is good to hear. Got some heavy thighs so people call me Zazz, which is short for Zassiccia, which is some kind of slang, means sausage in Italian.

Had clothes that was usually too big, especially my communion suit. My sister always said, "What a shame that kid had to go around with such a big suit. No wonder he went on drugs."

But most my clothes was strong, tough stuff, heavy duty. The kind of thing you find now in a Salvation Army. The kind of clothes make you feel like if you fall down you don't get too hurt.

Growing up in the neighborhood, there was safe all around. Lots of family for padding. Got a safe dad, he don't beat me, he don't go out getting drunk. Got a safe mom, she don't watch no soap operas or smoke cigarettes. Got no good reason for growing up and becoming a drug dope, except maybe that communion suit.

Got aunts and uncles say I'm a chubby baby, cute, and they twist my cheek while they make their own face go sideways in some kind of ecstasy, saying, "Oooh, what a little svoiardell."

Then when I'm older they say, "he's a handsome boy, Mary," to my mother, and then they twist my cheek some more while they make the same crazy face, and, "Oooh he's such a pasticceria!" All I know is it hurts.

I also got broken teeth. All my life I got either the left or the right front tooth broke. One time I did it trying to use a screwdriver like a crowbar to pry up some old nails in some old wood. Dad used the opportunity to give me one of his life rules, which I'll always remember — "the right tool for the right job."

The last time I lost one of them teeth was when all the drug chemicals I started taking made one of the roots swollen and then an old drunk dentist missed where he was supposed to drill and made a hole right through the top part of the tooth, so you could thread a string from one side to the other. This was wrong, so then he pulled it out altogether.

I got a brother and a sister, ten and nine years older then me. And we had a parakeet named Tony, who ate crackers off my chin when I was a baby. And a dog named Snoopy who was a puppy when I was one. And the giant rooster who sat out on the black wrought-iron front porch railing and made noise. The chickens, ducks and rabbits came and went usually around Easter, the same time dad's oldest brother, Uncle John, came around smoking cigars in a long grey overcoat. He looked like Edward G. Robinson, but he died from Parkinson's disease. I remember the last time he came to Lake Ronkonkoma with us he couldn't make a sandwich. His hands shook too much. But around Easter, before he died, he used to come with chickens or ducks or rabbits.

Dad's closest older brother, Uncle Carmine, and Aunt Jean Gremaldi, lived next door. Then next to them was Aunt Rose, dad's sister, and Uncle Joe, whose real name was also Carmine but everybody called him Joe so as not to mix them up, and also because Uncle Carmine didn't like him having the same name.

Uncle Joe set himself on fire one day when he squirted lighter fluid on the barbecue and the barbecue flame ran straight up into the can he was still holding and exploded. He looked pretty funny smacking at his chest, running all around the yard, till Uncle Carmine opened up the hose on him and drenched him, which Uncle Joe wasn't happy about either.

"Jeez, Carmine, why'd you do that, goddammit," Uncle Joe said, while his chest was still smoldering.

"You was on fire, fer cryin out loud."

"I woulda got it out."

"Next time I'll let you burn, okay, Joe?" And Uncle Carmine held the hose up to the side of his head and made a face like Uncle Joe was nuts. Us kids, us cousins, we laughed like crazy.

All this was happening when everything was dirt. Before cement. When all the aunts and uncles had a backyard that was one big backyard. No fences and no painted lawns yet.

There was a peach tree, a plum tree, a pear tree and a cherry tree, which was gigantic and hung way out over the roof of Uncle Carmine's garage. Us kids would climb the tree and eat the cherries. There was a grapevine that made a roof over a table in the place where we played cards and board games, and everything always got sticky from the grapes that were all the time falling. We'd eat them as they fell. The rest got turned into jelly or wine.

And there was fig trees! With fat figs. Purple. When you pulled them open they looked like blood inside. The fig trees got wrapped in burlap and thick black tar paper rolls every winter because they were delicate, and then they looked like halloween monsters sitting out there, sticking up at odd angles, all black and dark in the snow that covered everything else.

In the summer, there was two waves of cousins, some my brother and sister's age which meant nine or ten years older than me, and some, but not as many, around my age. Then there was neighborhood kids who mixed in besides. Us kids all ate dirt in the backyards and played war. "Bang, you're dead. I got you." "No you didn't." "Yes I did." "Bang" again, and somebody'd fall down all dramatic, like in the movies. War movies. They were big then.

Ozone Park was the neighborhood, where dad's dad, Santo, had made his claim, like Columbus coming over on a boat and saying, okay this is America.

Santo said, okay, too, this is mine. And then he sent his brother Uncle Zio back to Italy to get the wives, Aunt Zia and my grandmother, Marie, who I never met. Actually I never met Santo either, he died just about when I was born, but everybody says I got a lot of him in me 'cause we both like to wear vests.

And it was about that same time, when I was born, that dad took the dirt space between Uncle Carmine's and the original house Santo and Marie raised their family in, and he built a brick house, like one of the three little pigs did. And I grew up in it.

It was a nice house. Didn't have any cockroaches. Oh, maybe a waterbug or two once in a while. Squish 'em in the cellar. Was a dirt cellar. Just dirt. Down the basement steps from the hall by the kitchen, and you was on the dirt.

Till dad went and got linoleum. And celotex. And paneling. And turned the cellar into an Italian-American basement.

Italian-American Basement

The old cellar faded away piece by piece. Started when dad got himself all surrounded with a bunch of five gallon cans full of some kind of tar. And he spread it out in sweeps as long as his arm, with a trowel, dipping it in the can and lifting out what looked like black Turkish taffy, saying, "don't touch it 'cause it don't come off, get back." So I didn't do much.

Then came the linoleum. Stacks of squares in too heavy boxes for how small they were. Small like me. Dad had those boxes and me all around him. And I handed him one linoleum square at a time, thinking about how the brown and tan swirly design looked like mom's marble cake.

I looked at dad's back, kneeling down while he heated the linoleum squares with a torch and stuck them in the tar all over the floor. Dad worked good like this. He's built for it. Low to the ground and broad around the chest, with arms that work like heavy machinery. Powerful. And a bald head on top, so no hair falls in his face.

Dad worked bent on his knees like I seen him work hundreds of times. Got Italian knees, made with extra cushions for working on the ground. Dad got a lot of Italian in him, with an Italian name, Angelo, even though he's born American.

Later years, after the linoleum become part of our life, us kids couldn't roller-skate down there like we did when it was dirt (how'd we skate on dirt, I dunno) and whenever we did, mom got plenty infuriated because now it's the linoleum and we're screwing up the waxy shine getting marks all on it, and "this floor is supposed to be for good so quit your fooling around!"

It so happens that not one of them linoleum squares ever cracked or came up, not even peel in a corner, and it's been all my life so far. And to this day, mom is still waxing it.

Anyway, dad also covered over the green concrete walls down in the basement with paneling. Paneling was a big word back then. "Panel it," was what people said whenever they looked at something bumpy, or if it looked like old-fashioned, like old country, not new. Paneling was American.

And there was celotex for the ceiling. Cardboard boxes of celotex were dragged downstairs and I helped open them. These celotexes were like the linoleum, square and all ready to be stuck somewhere. Only they were lightweight. Reminded me of wafers. Reminded me of the host we got at communion in church on Sunday after confession on Saturdays. Big, giant, square hosts.

And I did like the priest did before he put one of them hosts on our tongues while we kneeled at the communion rail. I'd lift a celotex host, pass it through the air, slowly, saying, "nomina-padre-figlitu-spiritu-sanctum, amen" with each one I handed up to dad.

Till dad said, "what?"

And I said, "unh, unh," lifting my shoulders. We did this row by row, following the rows of lineolum squares below us, until the ceiling was covered.

Which by the way, the celotex ceiling's got some funny story connected to it, have to do with pea soup and mom's pressure cooker, and how dad every year repainted a big white circle on the celotex ceiling in the kitchen part of the basement because that's where the pea soup exploded and keeps bleeding through green. Pretty funny.

And mom got a new pressure cooker because — "Angelo, I had it on tight, the little gadget on the top was no good." Mom wiggles the little gadget with her finger. "See, the rubber seal is rotted," and she made a face like "Somebody Coulda Got Killed."

So dad told mom to go buy a new pressure cooker with the money he got doing house painting for other people. "But don't throw it away, Mary, I'll fix it." And mom never threw it away.

So most of the cellar got "finished," turned into an Italian - American basement, except for one part where there's a door, looks like a closet, and inside is all the old cellar. Got the old cellar smell and everything. Fat concrete walls all the time damp.

Inside is where dad keeps bottles of wine, all cool and dark, tucked in clink-clink together on some old wood shelves. Dark in a concrete corner. And there's a yellow light bulb on a quiet pull chain which don't interfere with the dark much at all, except make spiders stand still. I see them spiders vibrating though, their webs like springs.

And I got to use a chair, the only one that got left green when dad painted all the others. It sits in here all alone and stiff and cold. I stand on it but not for more than a minute just to look up on the high shelf, above the wine shelf, where the last year Christmas decorations go, and get myself scary because it didn't seem right all this color red and tinsel and the giant Santa face that usually goes outside on the front door upstairs. Down here it's horrible. In the wine cellar. Makes me feel like I got to pee.

And there's a safe in here. A gigantic box made of Kryptonite, I know, since some years later when I blossomed into a dope addict I tried to break the thing to get money which I figured dad kept in there. I tried a crowbar and everything but it never even blinked.

The safe came from an office building Uncle Carmine worked in. When the business moved out of town, somehow he got it, and then dad got it. I found out eventually that dad didn't even keep money in it, he used it to store away important house things like birth certificates and such. Funny thing about the safe is it's at least two times as big as the door. How'd it get in there?

Upstairs, in the kitchen is where relatives and friends go. Like Jimmy the egg man. Uncle Jimmy, who drove a round panel van, which he painted blue, with a regular paintbrush. He had an egg farm, or chicken farm, or some kind of farm and he was always in a hurry. He walked fast like chickens when you chase 'em. And he hurried in our driveway with cardboard cartons of eggs. Sometimes he'd sit and stay for coffee.

Or the Bea-un-ga-leen man (the bleach man), who was my mother's Aunt Amelia's son, I think. And who carried six, fat, gallon bottles, three of them in each hand, by hooking his thumb, his pinky and one other finger in the glass loops on the neck of the jugs. Six big fat bottles, what looked like pee. What'd mom use all that bleach for? He'd stop his delivering too, and sit and yak. Just like all the aunts and uncles, who stand up in the kitchen and talk with mom and dad. They usually drink some of mom's coffee which everybody always said stinks. Too strong. Mud. But mom just shrugs it off, she likes it that way. On Sunday they have a shot of whiskey. And more blah, blah, blah. And if it's summer, they go down the "finished" basement.

LaLa Jones

Lala wasn't his real name. Neither was Jones. Was Lawrence, Lawrence something. But we called him Lala.

Lala's a pretty tall guy. Lotsa leg. But all the time he's falling down, or into. Once Lala fell into a big glass window outside the Jamaica Avenue delicatessen, which is where everybody from the 106th Street park goes for food. Lala looked so funny sitting with the hams and the bolognas, and the crushed ice all mixed up with the broken glass. Lala got all cut up on that one but he didn't care. Lala just stays doped. Lala shoots so much heroin, he's never straight. Never.

Another time, Lala's doing okay. We're inside a supermarket on Liberty Avenue, was the A&P. Next thing I know Lala's not there.

"Hey, Lala." No Lala. Then I see feet sticking upside down from in the fish bin. Lala fell in with the fish. Too doped to get out.

"How'd you fall in there, you dope?" I say.

Lala just grins, upside down grin. "Dunno, gimme a hand will ya."

So I haul Lala out the fish tank.

"Let's get outta here, go get high," says Lala. Lala's already high as he's going to get. It's low from here on in.

So we go down the underground Long Island Railroad tracks

17

which runs underneath Atlantic Avenue. Way in on the cat-walk. This is a good place for doing dirty stuff. And we do more dope. Lala's so low now he forgets where we are, and he steps off the walk. He goes down like a plank. No arms out. Nothing. Just tips over sideways onto the tracks. And don'tcha know a train's coming.

"Lala, you best be getting up," I say, "a train's coming." Lala don't get up. But he moves a little.

"Gah," says Lala.

Oh, Lala's really in trouble now, I'm thinking. I try to fig-ure what to do, pretty doped myself, and brain cell activity mostly sluggish. Not like the train which is moving right along nice and perky.

Lala's too big to lift, no sense jumping down there with him. I get down flat and stick my hand down, feel around for some of Lala to grab. I get a coat collar. I pull. Lala's coming along. But so's the train. Long Island Railroad train moving real fast the closer it gets. But this don't matter much now, Lala's gonna be flat dead soon, fast or slow train.

"C'mon, Lala," I say.

Lala says, "lemme alone," and he yanks my hand free. Then the train arrives, right on time. I got to squish myself flat up verticle like, pancake to the wall, so's to keep me and the train from making any contact. It goes by forever and ever. Makes that forever noise trains make. Finally, I see a little red caboose light moving away fast. How many pieces Lala in? I wonder.

"Ho, gemme outta here," Lala says from down the track.

"Jeez," I say, "Lala you scared the hell outta me. How come you're in one piece?"

"Gemme outta here." Then I see Lala lying flat on his face in the little dip between the two tracks. Train went by–zip–right over Lala. Didn't touch him. But Lala's filthy since everything down here is black soot and mostly wet.

"Come on Lala, you can clean up at my house. Folks is out.

The sink in the basement's got hot water."

Lala hits the ground at least five times between the railroad and my house. He don't want to get up anymore. I drag him. He rips the knee in his pants. He leaves a shoe somewhere. And he stinks.

"Oh Lala, you some kind of pig mess."

"Yeah?" he asks, with a face that looks retarded.

In the basement I'm trying to help Lala get cleaned up. Cousin Frankie, next door, comes over since he seen us making a commotion in the alleyway.

Frankie says, "What happened to Lala?"

"Same old stuff," I say.

Frankie says, "you got any more dope?"

I say, "yeah, and it's good dope too." We both look at Lala, like Lala's proof of the pudding.

Frankie says, "you got gimmicks?"

I say "Lala got 'em." But the eyedropper we use for gimmicks, for shooting dope broke in Lala's pocket.

"What we gonna use to get off now?" Frankie's looking to me for an answer, even though Frankie is cousin Frankie who's a year older than me and in most our backyard growing up he always took the lead.

"Don't know, lemme think, too late to go to the drugstore to buy a new eyedropper." Frankie's staring at me with a little head nod. Frankie looks worried, but Frankie always looks worried. He's got more energy, don't know whether to call it nervous or worry or what, but he's got more of it than anybody in the entire world. And his red hair increases the intensity. Red hair. Him and his brother and his sister all got red hair. Italians with red hair! Crazy.

I'm looking back at Frankie, biting his nails. Frankie bites his nails real serious. Bites his skin too. When you look at Frankie he's usually got a finger in his mouth, chewing on it. And me and Frankie, we grew up so close, I know the smell of his wet skin.

Then I say, "we can use a Bic pen. Hollow plastic tube'll work good enough. We can stick a needle on one end, pacifier on the other. Do the trick just fine." I smile. Frankie's looking at me, skeptic-like.

So I say, "okay, I'll do it first, gimme yer belt." Frankie takes his belt off right away and helps me tie it on my arm. We're waiting for some veins to pop up.

"There goes one," I say. I poke at it with the needle. The vein wiggles to one side. I try it again, got it. Blood comes up in the Bic pen tube. "There, see." Frankie goes next.

Then Lala starts to move and mumble. Hard to shoot dope anywhere near Lala without him knowing it.

Lala says, "hey, lemme do some."

"Oh, jeez, Lala, you're a mess already."

"Come on, man, it's my needle," Lala says.

"Okay, okay," me and Frankie say, looking at each other like eyes up in our head.

Lala really trashing himself now. Keeps sticking the needle in his arm but keeps missing the vein. The needle ain't on the Bic pen thing too tight either. I'm waiting for the whole thing to fall apart.

Now Lala's arm is all dotted, red. Blood-like.

I say, "gimme, let me do it for you." I do. And Lala starts to tip over. Hits his head on the sink. Then straight down to the floor.

"Oh boy, Lala knocked himself out cold now," I say.

Frankie says, "Lala's always knocking himself out."

Frankie disappears behind the wine door. "Where's the light?"

"Feel around," I say, holding Lala's head a little up from the floor, like the wounded soldier thing in movies.

"It's cold in here," Frankie's hollering.

"You find the light?"

"No." I go in the wine room with Frankie. Frankie's looking to drink some wine, like in the good old days before we do all this drug stuff. I turn on the light and take a Progresso wine vinegar bottle that dad uses to cork up his red. Me and Frankie start drinking it right there, passing it back and forth. Frankie wants to lick the cork. I tell him, "no, I don't think mom and dad want your spit."

We come out and Frankie says, "let's listen to some records." And he feels his way over to the couch and falls on it. We listen to some old 45's. Fifties rock and roll stuff like the Platters and the Drifters.

"Good sound, huh?" says Frankie. He ain't biting his fingers.

"Yeah, real good sound."

So me and Frankie we're listening, and singing once in a while, sitting on a couch in the basement, where we used to roller-skate on the dirt floor before it got 'finished.'

We're leaning on each other. Feeling good. Till I notice Lala got blood dripping from his head. Making a red puddle on mom's linoleum.

"C'mon, let's get Lala up."

Frankie says, "okay," like his red jets are kicking in again and he needs to move. But Lala's like a big old sack of meat. Flops this way and that. We put ice cubes in Lala's underwear. We walk him around. Lala's feet just dragging along, got no power of their own.

Frankie looks at me, says, "why are we doing this? Lala's stupid and alla time ruining fun." So we drop Lala by the pool table. He sorta slides under it.

We decide to try and play some pool. But the pool balls don't go in the holes too good. Me and Frankie say, "whatsa matter with these balls?" And we quit. Then we see Lala's waking up.

"Lala, you got to go home," I tell him.

Lala says, "yeah, I gotta go home too." Lala don't know who's who and where's where.

Frankie asks me, "who's gonna carry him?"

21

"No problem, we get dad's car, the Rambler. Mom and dad over at Uncle Fuco's playing cards, pinochle, so they're good till midnight."

Frankie jumps and says, "hey, lemme drive."

I tell him, "Frankie, you don't know from drive."

Frankie says, "C'mon, it's easy." Frankie drives.

Oh boy, Frankie drives. Keeps missing lights, ignores stop signs, and don't even glance at the yields. Then we arrive on Lala's family's garbage cans and push 'em fast into his mama's rose bushes. "We're here," Frankie looks at me with some kind of pride. We're here all right and it looks like this where we stay. Old Rambler's dead. Just making a "rr . . . rr . . . rr," sound.

"Good work," I say.

Frankie says, "whatta we do now?"

"Pull the car out the bushes, put Lala on the porch, ring Mrs. Lala's bell, and then we walk home, that's what." And while I'm saying this I'm leaning over the seat pulling on Lala.

Lala's awake and he's fishing melty ice cubes out of his pants. He's still covered in soot. Still only one shoe. Still got ripped pants. Lala's one big confusion.

On the way home I say to Frankie, "Frankie, we got to do some fancy feet action with dad."

"Yeah!"

"We get back home and I'll call up Uncle Fuco's and ask dad if I can borrow the car to drive Lala home. Dad's a good guy and he'll probably say yeah, but come right home. But we're home already, see, Frankie?"

"Yeah, so then what?"

"So then we say, later, how the Rambler just went poop and we had to walk all the way home."

"Un-huh."

"Mom'll probably get suspicious all on her face but it'll be ok."

Frankie says, "yeah, good idea."

International House of Pancakes

The next day me and dad, and Frankie's dad, Uncle Carmine, we go on a Rambler safari to bring back dad's car.

We get an early start because Uncle Carmine's all huffy puffy about he ain't got all day. Far as I can tell, he's got all day, but he says he don't and that's that. Frankie's still snoozing, don't usually come out until dark.

Anyways, the three of us are in the front seat of Uncle Carmine's car, me in the middle. Uncle Carmine's thinking his dumb brother, Angelo, let his dumb son, Gregory, use his dumb Rambler, and now he's got to go all the way out to Hillside Avenue.

Uncle Carmine's not smiling. Got his hat on. Dad ain't too happy either. I got a tupperware bowl with some fried meatballs from last night that mom never puts in the sauce, she always makes a few like that. And I'm holding them up one at a time on a fork, taking bites all around from the center. Wish I was in the back seat.

We get to Lala's house and tie the Rambler to the bumper of Uncle Carmine's car. Uncle Carmine's not too happy about this. He only uses his car once, maybe twice a week. He uses the subway, the A train, to get to work in Manhattan every day. His car sits in his garage most of the time, nice and cozy, sleeping. It never had nothing tied on it's bumper.

Anyway, we're all set. I drive with Uncle Carmine. Dad's in the Rambler for steering and stopping. "Wagon Ho!" Uncle Carmine gives me a look like, this ain't funny.

Uncle Carmine don't say anything to me, and I don't say anything to him. Some things best left unsaid. I still got four meatballs left so I keep busy with that.

We're tugging along on Hillside Avenue. Come to a light. We stop. Dad stops. Uncle Carmine's staring straight ahead. I turn around and wave a meatball on a fork at dad. Dad's getting out of the Rambler. Uncle Carmine don't see dad get out. Dad walks up to Uncle Carmine's window, got something to say. Hi, dad, I'm thinking, too much meatball in my mouth to talk. Dad's making motions to roll down the window. But Uncle Carmine's still looking straight ahead. Got his hat tipped down low.

The light turns green. I watch Uncle Carmine put his shoe on the gas pedal. Uh, oh, I'm thinking. I turn around and see dad looking like, oh, my golly, better get back in the Rambler. He's running back. But Rambler's tied to Uncle Carmine's bumper, and it's got to follow Uncle Carmine wherever he goes.

Rambler's coming at dad, while dad's running at the Rambler. And the driver door's still open, just like he left it. Dad can't get around it, fast like. I got my mouth too full to tell Uncle Carmine that he'd better stop. Besides, if he stops now, Rambler's gonna smack him in the ass. Dad's hat blows off. He's running and bending at the same time now, trying to scoop up his hat. Good thing Uncle Carmine drives slow. Dad's car door bumps dad, real insulting like. That's it for dad, he gives up. But old Rambler don't give up. It's got momentum now. And it pulls to the right like always.

Uncle Carmine finally realizes what's going on, and he hits his brake hard. I'm thinking, Uncle Carmine, this ain't a smart thing to do, dad's Rambler's got nobody to step on it's brake. Sure enough, there goes Rambler, pulling to the right. Missed

Uncle Carmine's bumper by an inch. And like a dog on a rope, sprinting after a cat, reaches the end of the rope, and snap — Rambler's free.

Rambler goes sailing, nice and quiet like, across wrong way traffic. Lots of wrong way cars turning circles getting out the way. Looks like Rambler's headed for McDonald's. But it's still pulling to the right. Nice curve. And up a ramp it goes into the International House of Pancakes parking lot.

First it hits an Oldsmobile. Then it hits a Cadillac. Then it hits a big blue Buick, and then old Rambler's outta breath. Stops for a while. Then it starts rolling backwards, back down the ramp. But the front wheels are turned so much to the right, it just makes a nice as you please half circle, and comes to rest, perfect parallel park, alongside the curb. Beautiful.

Dad finally catches up. Uncle Carmine's yelling at dad, "why'd you do that?" Dad's all out of breath himself, ducking and dodging wrong way traffic, just like his Rambler, only dad had a kind of jerky motion, Rambler was smooth, didn't hesitate once. He yells at Uncle Carmine, "why'n't you open yer window?"

People coming out of the House of Pancakes now likes ants storming a sugar cube left out in the sun. Everybody's pointing and yelling. I'm eating real fast now. Taking lots of small bites, turning the fork around and around. I try hard not to laugh, I know this ain't funny. And I choke and laugh till I die.

No doubt this is a terrible mess. And I feel bad for dad and for Uncle Carmine, and for all the pancake people with dents in their cars, but like dad's Rambler, I'm outta control.

Next day dad's trying to explain to the insurance man how a four car pile-up, with no drivers, can happen. I'm looking at dad from in the kitchen. He's on the phone in the dining room. Mom's behind me cooking at the stove, but she's listening to what's going on. It don't make sense to her, the car stuff. But she knows something else. Something more important. Her boy is up to no good, and down to dirty business, lying.

Dad does some scribbling on a piece of paper, makes a diagram like the insurance man says. Looks like a football play, far as I can tell. Dad ain't happy at all. He's giving me the look like, what's the matter with you, this how I brought you up? The lead in the pencil breaks. But he's done writing anyway. He turns his head the other way, his back to me.

I'm looking at dad's hand on the telephone. Big hand. Strong, honest hand. Dad got honest hands. And I think about dad's dad, Santo, the picture of him standing in his garden, with his vest on, with big wide honest hands holding onto a tomato stick.

I'm s'posed to somehow be a lot like Santo, my grandfather, even though he died the year before I was born. I look at my hands. Stupid hands. I'm looking at the back of dad's head. Big bald spot. Strong head. I'm thinking, I'm a dumb head. Wish Santo was around, I'd apologize.

Beach

Lots of cousins, kids, we all go to the beach. Rockaway Beach. Big fun. Hot tea and coffee with milk. And jelly doughnuts in the sand by mom's or dad's or somebody else's beach chair. We come out wet and soggy what otherwise would have been sweat from so much wrestling and crazy. Fun in the wavy water, splash! And sticky with sand by the time we get to the blanket where whoever took us got the beach chairs. Got a goofy umbrella on occasions when there's lots of family. Or for some other reason, who knows?

We stand around shivering from the chill, all us kids attached to each other by grabbing on to one towel. Got it across our backs, and we bump into each other. Cold skin. Almost knock each other down when one grabs too much to get it across his front.

We can't wait while dad pours hot from the thermos and mom or Aunt somebody gives out the jelly doughnuts. Yum! Um... Can't tell sand from the sugar sprinkle till you crunch your teeth and it don't melt. We go from shivering to running again soon as we get even half through eating the doughnuts.

"Don't go in the water!" they yell at us, since jelly dough-nuts make you drown if they're too soon in you and you step in the ocean. So we go run out on the jetty. And look behind us for the umbrella, or dad's hat. Dad always wears a hat. He's got a few and they're all called Angelo hats.

We look behind us since we're scared to death of the black, oily, shell-covered jetty which seems to breathe and move when the waves swell up on it and cover it with green foam. Before one wave goes away another one comes and makes it more swollen. Then more green. Prehistoric.

How we get to the beach is usually with dad. Dad had a round old car. Black. Like an Elliot Ness Untouchables car. Called it "Nellie Bell," which was the name of a race horse. Had a grey felt lining on the inside, and a seat like on the old A train subway car. Pack all us kids in the back. Don't worry about seat space, just pile in on top of each other. Lots of touch. Kids like that.

After we quit fighting for a window, which in old Nellie Bell only goes down half way, we commence to comparing body parts for the ride.

"Lookit, he got a little dink."

"I ain't got a little dink, you got a little dink."

"Lookit, yours comes to a point." And somebody snaps somebody's bathing suit, "ow, leeme alone."

"Hey, you got round knees."

"You got square knees."

"Yaa! You got knock-knees."

"No I don't."

"Yeah, yeah, yeah. Look at 'em."

And then somebody raps somebody else on the knee with a knuckle fist to make a reflex happen, so they'll kick the back of dad's seat and he'll say something.

So anyways, off the block we go, to Jerome Avenue. Then Crossbay Boulevard which gets real wide and lots to look at since we ain't in Ozone Park no more, we're in another neighborhood. Howard Beach. And for us kids this is like Christopher Columbus. We argue about who discovered the Ozone Park neighborhood.

"Was Ponce de Leon."

"No, Francisco de..."

"What?"

"The guy who discovered Incas."

"You don't know what you're talking about."

"So what?"

"So this."

And somebody gets somebody in a head lock. And somebody else pulls his toes apart.

"Quit it. That hurts."

"Hey, cut it out back there."

"Baby."

Soon comes the old-old-old-old-old Hamilton Beach bridge. Made out of wood. Cars don't go on it anymore because it's creepy. And sad. But people walk on it.

The other side of the Hamilton Beach bridge we only look at from the Nellie Bell window. Till we get older and able to ride bikes across streets and can get there by ourselves. To go fishing and crabbing and creeping and crawling all under and around, and looking for the spot where somebody jumped off for swimming but got his head stuck in the mud and died, because there's all this mystery about sandbars and "don't you kids ever go swimming in there!"

We pass by the Hamilton Beach bridge and over the Howard Beach bridge we go in Nellie Bell. Lots of people fishing off the side. Got stone railings, and metal in some places. The metal part's some grid we can see through to the water below, which makes us real uncomfortable to look at. And the car tires make a woooooo sound, which is also scary but dad convinced us we won't die even if the bridge falls apart since Nellie Bell's built like a submarine.

On the other side it's nothing but a long straightaway with high grass and swamp and a bird sanctuary on both sides. And there's an all steel bridge way out in the water past the birds and the high grass and the swamp. Way out in the middle of the water. It's a train bridge. The A train that clunks and clanks all the way from the Bronx, through Manhattan, through Brooklyn, then Queens and now it's running right along parallel with us. So far out that we can't hear it. But we pace Nellie Bell.

"C'mon Nellie Bell." And we're jumping up and down to make Nellie Bell go faster.

"C'mon, dad. It's beatin us, go faster." But dad absolutely don't go faster. And sooner or later the train's lost behind the high grass again. So we start a dumb game with other car's license plates. Looking for one from China. Most we ever see is a New Jersey.

This is the longest part of the drive. This Africa Avenue. Young people with their cars go crazy here. Like there's no rules no more. They speed their cars because it's far away and alone. And in all my life I ain't never seen a police car here. Once in a while you see a dead car with rust and no wheels and usually garbage around it. Every time we go to the beach and pass it there's more garbage and less car.

Soon comes Broad Channel. Another neighborhood. Now we're getting closer to the beach because here people live in houses half in the water. Built up on poles. Talk about crazy. And stores (not many) all got the word "sea" in it somehow. There's one place we all wait for. It's a house in the water with shrunken heads on the roof. And one shrunken head closer to the road on a pole. We don't know why. It's just there.

"Probably voodoo."

"... yeah."

"Don't stop the car, dad. Don't get no flats!"

But the most unusual part of the ride is the Broad Channel bridge. With a toll. And us kids wrestle for the left side window right from the start to throw the dime in the basket. If we're just in Nellie Bell then one of us gets to throw the dime, and the thing goes up, ding and we go through. But if we're more than one car, more than one dad family caravan then one of the dads gives money to a policeman in a booth, like at the movies, and the policeman waves us all through by how many dimes.

Then comes the most excitement. At the Broad Channel bridge there's a drawbridge. And it's big. Bigger than we can see across. Partly since it's got hills and turns but also, it's BIG. And we pray that the bridge is going up when we get there. Don't happen a lot but when it does, "wow, wow, wow!"

First, a bell's dinging. And road blocks drop down, to stop cars. Then the ding, ding, ding's going in time with the whole floor ahead of us breaking apart and lifting up. UP! It splits in two, all metal. And gets gigantic.Turns into a wall. Scary up close. Real scary. Then we all got eyes out for the boat, coming from one side or the other. We know it's out there, and we're frantic who's going to spot it first.

"There it is. There it is!"

"I seen it first."

"Where?"

"Inna ocean, stupid."

"Lookit, it's gonna hit."

"Naw, it ain't gonna hit, you dopey or what?" And it don't hit. It never hits. Just sinks away from us on one side, then shows up later on the other side going away, headed for the railroad bridge. We never see what happens to it there since we're gone by then. But the bridge's got to deflate first. And this takes a long time which ain't so much fun and, "c'mon, c'mon, c'mon."

So anyway, up on the bridge we go. Then turn some and wind down till we come off the real bridge part. But somehow it ain't real street yet. In fact it ain't never real street on this side of the bridge because there's sand drifted everywhere. And sand is all confused in with the roadside dirt. And then sand only. Then the boardwalk.

"We're here!" And us kids in the back seat like puppies climbing on each other with no where to go because we still got to park.

"C'mon, dad, park."
"Hurry, I gotta pee."
"You can pee in the water."
And we do.
Ocean.

The DeWayne Tragedy

Somewhere around the middle of the sixties, when I was a flowering adolescent, drugs were good. Like fun. I fell in love with that LSD drug, and all its chemical relatives. Loved to walk around in circles for hours, sometimes days, in some sort of altered metamorphic mental condition. Sometimes I didn't move at all.

I took a lot of them screwy head chemicals, mixed up with speed drugs, and got a reputation like, wow-wee-wow, devil may care, high-wire crazy boy. But still a good boy. Nice boy. Didn't do no harm. Least it seemed that way.

Met up with DeWayne then. DeWayne's just getting introduced to fun drugs. He's got this intellectual interest in psychedelic experiments. DeWayne got one of them receding heads, looks like more head than hair. Makes him look smart, big dome-like. He's got a little face, with glasses. Round ones. And he dresses so college. Like Kingston Trio college. Like very conservative college. Fact is, he's a college boy. Studying that psycho-logic stuff at some funny sounding place, Adeline, Adelfine, Adlehead Universe City, or something like that.

I go to school too, for art, but I don't wear no college boy accoutrements like DeWayne. I got stripe pants and bare feet and big hair, and hats. Funny hats sometimes. It ain't above me to dress up now and then like some character in a book. Giles, the Goat Boy once. Cotton pasted all on my face, big furry feet, no hooves though.

DeWayne giggles a lot at this kind of stuff. He giggles so hard, his glasses slip down his nose. All the time he kicks them back up with a finger. And giggles them back down again.

I like DeWayne because he's smart. And because he giggles. And because he went and got this red car. A Bug. First person I know took out a loan to buy a new car. Cost him one thousand, eight hundred and fifty dollars. I remember. And it was red, red, red. A little Volkswagen. He giggles even more now.

DeWayne does this funny thing with the Bug car. He aims the window wash up high. When he hits the button, water squirts clear over the little red roof, and he gets somebody wet behind him. He giggles so hard when he does that, can't even talk.

DeWayne plays the guitar. Nice. Like Peter, Paul and Mary. And Judy Collins. And who I like most, Joni Mitchell. He makes a special face when he plays, but his glasses don't slip down then. They stay put when he's playing his guitar. Serious.

DeWayne's guitar is almost as big as DeWayne. Least as wide. And it fills up the whole back seat of his Bug car. Perfect.

Me and DeWayne, we take lots of LSD. But me more than him. This is about when I start to reach some kind of saturation point with all my drug chemical ingestion, like too much sugar in a glass of water, only it ain't sugar, it's cocaine and methamphetamine sulfate — speed — and LSD hallucinogenics. And the result of this type of saturation is I start to feel a little bit part-time psychotic, and sometimes schizophrenic.

Since all this velocity and hallucination is becoming a nuisance, I start eyeing up dead drugs. Tranquilizers, barbiturates, and horrible, horrible heroin. I'm keeping this type of down drug food handy for when I need lazy day retirement time. Got to. Got to since I can't rely on plain old going to sleep anymore, it don't always happen.

And got to because funny things are happening at home. Like not being a hundred-percent sure if it's me turning the toilet bowl water blue, as if maybe psychedelic color somehow's become a part of my body fluids.

Or time when we're all sitting at the kitchen table, and I can't remember if we just finished eating or we just getting started.

So I start taking some serious slowpoke drugs, for sleep and for nervous. DeWayne don't do that. He's only interested in psychedelic experiments. So far.

DeWayne goes someplace else when I take narcotic drugs. I never see the someplace else. DeWayne got a mom, but I never see her. DeWayne got high education palsies, but I don't see them either. I only see DeWayne, one side. DeWayne only wants to see me, one side.

The times DeWayne takes his own LSD, he's comparing, and this works out okay for me because he makes the whole abnormal and alterational experience have some science to it, which I like. But then the eventual happens and DeWayne starts to drift into speed drugs, like cocaine and methadrine, which he starts to do contrary to any of his plans, but that's the inevitable part of drug taking, you almost never take just one drug and go away satisfied.

When DeWayne does this he ain't so much fun. He gets too skinny looking, and talks too much no-talk. Way far away talk. So far, he can't keep up talk. And he gets himself confused, then unhappy. Which is why DeWayne then starts asking me for some down, down down drugs. More of the unavoidable part of being in a drug career.

Like night follows day, down drugs follow up drugs. Even when you're just an apprentice in drug work. It's an almost necessary thing to do, unless you're willing to feel so poor, so much like garbage, like beyond the planet of under the weather from the rebound aftereffect of speed drugs that it more than undoes the fun part. No bargain. Bad deal. Like working for no pay, almost. Only worse. Like paying to go to work, and at work you get hurt, or something crummy like that.

So DeWayne takes some down dead drugs because he got himself too wiery from speed drugs, which he shouldn't a took in the first place. But DeWayne gets all drunk-like on down drugs. Gets a big dopey smile, trips and bumbles all over the place. Gets in his Bug car and drives on people's lawns, and squirts them. This makes me laugh, but deep inside it makes me sad. Because DeWayne don't belong here. He don't belong dopey. DeWayne's best on LSD, and that's all.

Then one day, me and DeWayne was sitting on a park swing, swinging. He's talking to me about people either being "do" people or "be" people. And he hands me this licked letter. He says, "please, Gregory, open this tomorrow afternoon and do what it says inside." Then he shows me a big bunch of red pills. "Gonna swallow these," he says, "won't be here no more."

I look at DeWayne, he's not giggling. He's smiling though. Far away smile. Don't know where it is, smile. But it's got love all in it, I can tell. I'm thinking, that DeWayne, he's beautiful.

"Okay," I say, "I'll do that." Next day I go to school. Art school. I carry a big black portfolio. Got art, art stuff, drugs, and DeWayne's letter inside. I do some drug dealing up at school. I get good drugs from friendly school connection, a mix of fun drugs and dead drugs, then I sell what produce I don't want, and what I can afford to be without. Keep some for me. Keep dead drugs for me. Business.

This is a time when I was at a crossroad. Still with the peace and love bunch. With happy, fun drug people. But beginning to creep in dark corners. Creeping where dead drugs live. Creeping where heroin runs like rats in the garbage. Creeping like a hungry rat. Act like some kind of middle person — go creeping, bring home rat drugs and fun drugs, then sell some of both to good boys and girls. But they ain't really so good, they just don't go creeping, is all. Not yet.

Then I go home to a good mom and dad and try and pretend that I'm still a good boy. But the illusion is getting thin in both places. Hard to get the creeping rat stink off. Not like fun drugs don't have any smell either, just easier to conceal.

Also, about this time, I start using needles to shoot dope, and other drugs. Just was a logical progression. Sniffing drugs up a sore old nose don't speak of efficiency at all. Nose getting all bloody from harsh chemicals eating at the insides. Swallowing drugs simply works too slow. Not efficient.

Smoking drugs, you waste a lot. And it ain't too strong either, (this is before smokable chemicals like crack, cocaine and brown smokey heroin come to the neighborhood.) So, a needle's . . . the right tool for the right job, as dad always said. But I don't use a needle just for heroin dead drugs. I'm still crossing over and got a lot of psycho mental alteration love left, so I also shoot up LSD.

Times shooting up LSD are extraordinary, and very looney. LSD starts making needle marks look like big gaping holes. And holes start to move around. Hallucinate them getting big and small, big and small. They get so big they nearly swallow me up. Scary. Scary needle holes come to life like the brooms did to Mickey Mouse when he was the Sorcerer's Apprentice.

And the whole business of using heroin got all this negative bad karma and stigma attached, and rapid-fire LSD got a way of highlighting this beyond any ability to use blinders. So the voice of logic, or common sense as dad used to put it, takes me by the arm and tells me to knock off the looney LSD stuff and get some feet planted in the ground.

"How I do that?" I ask the voice. And the voice says, "Heroin the best medicine for all illness." Which, of course, is true. It don't necessarily make hallucinations go away, but it makes it so, who cares? Like as if it's all some sit-onna-couch-watching-a-tv-show.

"What about the bad karma? The bad dope junkie thing?" But the voice only says, "old wives tale, wadda they know." And this is true because, for sure, none of my family, teachers, nuns or priests ever use any heroin, so how they know?

So anyway, I'm coming home from school. Late afternoon. Walking the four blocks from the A train on Liberty Avenue, to home, on the other side of Jerome Avenue. I'm thinking about DeWayne I'm thinking how if he did what he said he was going to do, he'd be dead by now. I start to wondering how he feels being dead.

Get to the corner of my block, our house is in the middle. I see DeWayne's Bug parked out front. I'm thinking, why'd he do that? He dead inside. Why'd he do that here? But when I get up to the car, no DeWayne inside. Maybe he's left the car to me. Feel bad. The Bug car'd be nice to have, but I don't want no dead DeWayne.

I go in the house. DeWayne's there, talking to my mom. The two of them, nice as you please. DeWayne smiles, "Hi, Gregory."

"Hi, DeWayne, here's your letter back." DeWayne smiles some more. Big old DeWayne grin. Pushes up his glasses. My mom starts to hurry up some spaghetti for me. DeWayne's already got a dish. While mom's at the stove, DeWayne asks me, "Gregory, did you read my letter?"

"Nope, not supposed to till after."

"You want to read it?"

"Nope, it don't count no more." Then I say, "glad to see ya." DeWayne smiles. Then DeWayne asks me, "you got any dope?" This surprises me. It sounds funny coming from DeWayne. From his smart head, all big and brainy.

"Yeah, I got dope." Fact is, I got dope all the time now. Makes me feel good to have dope. So after I do some, still got more.

DeWayne says, "can I do some with you?" I look at him funny. I want to say, no, it ain't good for you, DeWayne. You better off without it. But this sounds silly to me. DeWayne starts getting up. He lifts the chair backwards nice and gentleman like. "Bye, Mrs. Gregory," he hollers to my mom who went down the basement. "Thank you for the spaghetti, it was terrific," he rubs his belly and makes a full face. Then to me he says, "Got to get home now, see ya later. You'll have dope later, right?"

"Okay," I decide.

Later, DeWayne comes over. DeWayne says, "hello, Mrs. Gregory." I hear my mom say, "hello DeWayne, can I get you something to eat?" Mom likes DeWayne. He's got respectable all over him. Plus, he looks like maybe he should eat some more since he's built small. Mom tries to feed him again.

My dad says, "leave 'em alone, Mary," and he smacks his stomach, like lookit what's happened to him.

"Just a little something, some meatballs?" mom says.

"No, thank you," says DeWayne, big smile, little giggle. But food's coming anyway, so I hustle DeWayne out the door.

"Gotta go, ma, no more food."

DeWayne's saying, "you got wonderful parents."

I say, "I know." We don't talk about the letter or what DeWayne did with the suicide pills. Or why he changed his mind about doing it. But DeWayne's bugging me still about the dope thing.

"Okay, okay," I say, "but you snort it. You don't shoot it." DeWayne agrees to this. He's snorted speed drugs before so it won't be the first time his nose gets asked to do this kind of thing. And I feel okay since he don't use a needle and heroin, both the same time, first time.

DeWayne gets his nose all ready. Trying to look at it like it's some kind of instrument. A funny sight. So serious. And he snorts. Then he holds his head back like he just took some nose drops. Then he comes forward, in slow motion. His eyelids like pillow cases. And then he gets good and sick. Throws up. But this is natural. First time anybody I know take heroin, usually they get sick to their stomach. Later, he ain't sick. Feels good.

DeWayne wants to take heroin dope more times after that. Three more times that week. Then DeWayne wants to try a needle. Skin pop. At first I argue. But he says, "you do it." Which is true. So I do it for him. I put a needle in his leg. Then he wants to mainline dope. Direct, in a vein.

"Want to do it to the fullest," he says. And he looks at me so much in the eye, like of course I know exactly what he's talking about and how can I possibly argue with him.

DeWayne and me we go upstairs in my bedroom. DeWayne takes off his belt. "Use my belt," he says. Nice belt. Suede. Soft on the arm. I go first. DeWayne watches the ritual, all full of curious. He don't flinch at the blood. Then I do DeWayne. He's talking all the while. Asking me, "what next? what next? what next?" Next, DeWayne goes straight back on the bed.

I say, "DeWayne?" DeWayne don't say much. I enjoy the dope feeling for a while. Then I say, "DeWayne?" DeWayne still don't say much. In fact, DeWayne don't move. "Uh, oh, look like you overdose, DeWayne." But DeWayne don't hear me. I slap DeWayne some. It don't do nothing. He just flops with the slap.

I go down to the kitchen, get some salt. Mom and dad are in bed now, after watching the eleven o'clock news. I go back upstairs, mix up salt and water and shoot it in DeWayne. Don't know why but this always seems to work on people when they overdose. Something I learned in the drug business. But nothing happens. I go back downstairs and get a bunch of ice. This don't work either.

I say, "DeWayne, DeWayne, DeWayne." DeWayne starts leaking foamy blood out the side of his mouth. "Uh, oh." I go downstairs, talk into mom and dad's dark bedroom. "DeWayne fell asleep and won't wake up."

Next I remember, DeWayne is laying peaceful like at the bottom of the stairs that lead up to my room. Police in the house. Ambulance in the house. Hands going up and down all over DeWayne. DeWayne's dead.

The next morning, DeWayne's mom is on the phone saying to me that she'll drop the homicide charges *if I stay away from the funeral!* I say, "sure, Mrs. DeWayne."

After that DeWayne's belt is hanging on my closet doorknob. I wear it. That's the end of DeWayne. I don't see him all dressed up with flowers. I don't see him all close eyed in the coffin. I just got DeWayne's belt.

Then one day I come home from school. Walk in the kitchen. Mom's cutting up food, crying. I say, "what's wrong?"

She says, "I loved DeWayne." I hold mom. Smell old tears and feel her short breath. I hold mom some more. Don't know what else. Don't cry, far as I can remember. Fifteen years later I cry.

Nanine's

Nanine made me drunk. Her size, her smell. The room full of scrap cloth and spools of colored thread. And the hard cardboard boxes with their tops all off, spilling over with tiny metal hooks, pins and snaps. Gold and silver. And sometimes shiny black. Like pirate treasure.

The darkness of her house, her room. Nanine was always in her room, in her chair. Nanine'd fill up the whole chair. Become the chair. Mom was big next to me but she shrank when we got to Nanine's. I was maybe five, six years old.

We'd walk down some steps, broken concrete. Me and mom. And I'd look for a doorbell, but mom'd just walk in. "Come on, stop your dillydallying." I always wished we'd knocked or something. Prolong the getting inside.

The getting inside. The predictable dark. Like my closet at night. Or under my bed when the house was asleep. Or like the black alleyway behind D'Argenzio's Meat Market. All those places I wasn't going unless somebody was with me. And maybe not even then. They always made me feel like I had to pee.

And I always felt like I had to pee when I got to Nanine's. The whole time we was there I'd squeeze the front of my pants and move my legs. I think mom felt it too because soon as we got home she'd run into the bathroom.

Nanine's smell didn't help. Nanine smelled like Italy. Like

cheese. The same smell I got at Nanine's I got at Russo's Cheese Store. Russo's Cheese Store had giant cheeses wrapped in big heavy ropes hanging from the ceiling. Silver hooks in the metal ceiling. The giant cheeses had hard waxy skin with red ink letters stamped on them. Looked foreign. They was bigger than me from head to toe. And soon as you'd look up at 'em, which you had to do, all the cheeses started to sway as if you was on a boat. I swear. And the floor was hardwood with sawdust an inch thick on it, so I'd slide my feet when I walked in. And Russo's had a big white display counter. Gigantic. Enamel and glass all around three sides of the store. Russo all the time moving around behind it. In his white paper hat. Reminded me of a shoot 'em down duck in an arcade game. Down below, through the glass display windows, where Russo's knees were, there was porcelain trays full of artichoke salads and black olives and tripe and hearts and . . . Lord, oil! Everything was drenched in olive oil.

But Russo's didn't so much smell like Nanine. It was Nanine smelled like Russo's. The cheeses and the oil. It was Nanine. Had to be since there was nothing else at Nanine's that owned any real smell worth taking note of. Nothing but sacks and bags and heaped-up tons of materials and sew stuff. And rolls of piping. This soft cotton rope stuff. Came in colors. We'd end up with lots of leftover piping. Dad used the odd pieces to tie up his tomato plants. And to bundle up stacks of old newspapers. I grew up with this stuff. Was all over the place. I still got some now. Almost two hundred miles and more than thirty years away. There's pieces tied to my tomato sticks from last summer.

Anyway, none of that stuff smelled once we got it out from Nanine's. Got it out and took it all home, for mom to do her work. All the bows and knots and wheels and buttons and loops she made with the piping. All small. No bigger than one of my fingers. She made shopping bags full of them. I'd play around with them thinking, what'd Nanine want all these for? Till mom used a few on a blouse she'd made for herself. Then I got the picture. A little knot and a little loop. Held needle and thread tight to opposite side of the blouse. One goes through the other.

Mom got so many pennies apiece. And I threaded needles. I tried to do the knots but my fingers got all twisted and red. Too many ins and outs, and tugs and loops. Mom wore a thimble to push the needles through them knots. It was hard. Few times I tried it, the thimble fell off and the backside the needle stabbed me. Flesh gave way before the knot did. But this didn't seem to happen to mom. Least she never made no pain noise.

Same like with the burns on her forearms from ironing. And on the backs of her hands from inside the oven. She never wore gloves when she reached in the oven. How'd she do that? Asbestos fingers? Anyway, no voice of pain.

Mom had a spot she worked in, in the parlor. A chair set up close to an end table by the couch. Table was small. Round. Had an old-fashioned Italian lamp on it right in the middle. The lampshade was a beige underwear-like material. Stretched taut. I'd stick my threaded needles into it. Line them up in a row. And when they came out they didn't leave any holes.

I sat on the couch. We both had an angle of the tv from our corner. The tv glowed grey. This was before color.

"What a good boy," she'd say to me. "Little love, do the next one double-threaded. And no more brown."

"No more brown?"

"How many have you got? Ten? No more brown. You can do some yellow next."

And then mom'd start to hum her never-ending medley. Pick up anywhere and stick one song into another. Didn't matter. Like a string of pearls, no beginning, no end. Stop anyplace, and gaze. It was her lifelong song. She'd hum. And "la-la, di-di, da." I'd always know mornings by the sound of her "da-da, di-di, da . . . hum-humm. Say you love me true, hum-humm.

Honey but it's true . . ." And the glass coffee pot and water in the sink. Mom in the kitchen. Morning!

But in the parlor she'd get herself all set up. With a low-cut cardboard box filled with her spools of thread. Which I fished around in for the right color. And brown grocery bags, one for the finished pieces and one for the mates to those pieces. And more grocery bags about to split from the cardboard spools of the piping. The spools had all they could hold, fat plump in the middle so the stuff don't slip off the sides. And I whittled them down cutting off lengths which I measured against a yardstick on the rug. And I draped them over the arm of the couch.

The leftover empty spools I collected. Gonna do something with them, but I don't think I ever did anything 'cept roll them all over the house. So the empty spools and the full ones, and the brown grocery bags filling up, and the box of threads, and the threaded needles, all surrounded mom. The Italian lamp a reflection in her glasses. This was her homework. Nanine would give it for her to do.

What'd mom think about then? Her song was only an accessory. Spilled out thoughtlessly. Talking to me couldn't have been much. And the sewing was easy as breathing, it looked. So what else was going on? Maybe mom was thinking about next day's meal plans. What to buy for dinner. What's on sale at Gelatos? Or what to do with what she had. Meals took plans back then. This mighta been before tin foil even.

What else? What else could mom been thinking of? Her mother? Grandma? She walked over there a lot. Two and a half blocks on the other side Jerome Avenue. She went there and did things. Mom was the second-oldest of ten. And there was seven brothers. Those Italian brothers, they expected things. Mom was a mom almost all her life. Apprentice.

So maybe mom was thinking about her brothers. Or maybe about art. I remember them uncles always saying, "oh, that Mary, she could draw." But they'd smile and rub their tummys and say, "and cook." Mom told me herself how she liked art in high school but had to quit school to go work in a button factory. She was good at art but there was no money in it. Making buttons in a factory got you so much money for so many buttons. Simple, I guess. So maybe mom thought about art.

Or maybe she was thinking about dad. If dad wasn't working nights he'd be there in his dad chair. Opposite the couch. But he worked nights and didn't get home till one in the morning. And I don't think dad liked Nanine. So mom got as much work done before he came home, I think, 'cause somehow there'd be no trace of any of it in the morning. Somehow it got all put away. I don't remember seeing it happen, but then I'd usually fall asleep on the couch.

In fact, was part of dad's routine soon's he come home to carry me upstairs to bed. So they tell me. And that was how he got his hernia. I don't think this was really true. One of them family joke things. I was the heaviest though.

Anyway there was no trace of Nanine in the parlor by the morning, so maybe that's what mom thought about while her hands did all that work. Getting so much done and put away before dad came home.

On weekends though dad would come home with bagels. Hot bagels. Fresh from the bagel factory. He'd stop and pick them up on his way home from the Post Office. Dad worked in the Post Office. He used to work in a candy factory, before I can remember. And I think he invented chocolate. Or some kind of bar. Baby Ruth maybe. But dad took the post office job when mom was pregnant with my sister, Maryann. My brother, Louis, was already around. I didn't happen yet. There was the war then too. But all that stuff gets fuzzy to me. Candy bars, war, button factories.

In any case, dad turned down an executive position in the candy place to get security in the post office. And on the way home on weekends he picked up bagels. I'd fight to stay awake, waiting. Watch Zacherly on tv do his crazy stuff in between the Mummy or Frankenstein Meets Somebody. Watch with my sister, and we'd scratch each other's backs. But she was older and sometimes did homework. My brother was fun to laugh at Zacherly with if he was there. 'Cause he was even older and been outside the house and had experience. But my sister was who protected me from the Mummy.

Then just when Zacherly ended, dad came home. With a dozen or so of them bagels. Sweltering. Butter melt just being near them. And cream cheese, and tea. Steamy tea with milk. Cold milk for dad. Dad rejoiced in cold milk. It was one o'clock in the morning. No one else in the universe existed. Not even Nanine.

In the daytime everybody's gone. Brother and sister in school and dad's sleeping. So mom's finishing some last minute pieces in the kitchen. I kneel on a chair with my elbows on the table. Pick at breakfast remains.

Then mom packs everything into a wide body shopping bag with rope handles. And I get out of my flannel pajamas and slipper-sox, and into pants with elastic, sneakers and a polo shirt. And we go walk on Jerome Avenue to Nanine's.

We don't do much talking. Not like I remember anyway. I look in store windows and count cracks in the sidewalk. And start timing my steps from a half block point to the corner. See if I can get either one of my feet to land right on the edge of the curb. Usually got to cheat some.

At the corner mom grabs my hand and I sail off the curb. Crossing the street I look down at the black. A lot of good things flattened in the tar, melted by the summer. I try to bend and scoop at anything metal but mom's got my hand too high. I always end up in a hop, till we reach the other side.

"Walk nice, will you. Don't pick up that junk." Mom's other hand a white fist from the weight of the shopping bag.

We walk from 104th Street where we live, to 98th Street, which is where I lose direction. On ninety-eighth we turn. Can't see Jerome Avenue no more. And then we're at Nanine's!

Nanine's house had red roof shingles on the sides. Roof shingles. And they were old and all chipped. The black tar paper showed underneath. And we go down them busted steps. Dark. Darker. Then the smell was there. And we walk into it.

Soon as we get inside mom puts down the shopping bag. I grab it. Hold on to the hot rope handles with both fists. Got the bag so it's in front of me. Got the tops of my sneakers under it. Anchored. While mom takes a handful of pieces out from the top of the bag and a piece of paper she got straight-pinned to the side of the bag. It's got her count on it. So many knots. So many loops.

Nanine got a nub of a pencil. And she got it in her teeth – gums, really, I don't remember teeth – while her arms come up from a big lap. Big rolling-pin arms. Looks like mom's bread dough. Heavy and pasty. And they move like they don't even belong to her. They move. Draw things in close to her. And the fingers wiggle. Nothing else moves. Nanine don't stand up. Only bends forward once or twice, which makes huge dough rolls bulge from inside her dress. Thin old house dress, like a worn curtain.

What do they talk about? Nanine don't talk to me. Nanine don't speak English. But they speak. What? What? This ain't barter. Nanine got her prices set. Mom accepts that. I think it's how much new work Nanine gonna give over. Mom wants the work. But Nanine got to make some fuss first. They talk choppy Italian.

"Nodo, nodo."

"Bottone."

"Mal equilibrato." But fast, "malequilibrato," Nanine says as she shakes and pulls one of mom's nodos apart.

I'm scared. Afraid if Nanine gets any more upset she'll stink so the roof might cave in. But I look at mom and she's okay. Mom's nodding, with sincere on her face. Puts up with Nanine's fat nitpicky. And she takes back whatever Nanine's finger mauling. Then she turns for the bag. I got to let go 'cause mom lifts the bag over close to Nanine and holds it open. Nanine's got it in close. Between her legs. Nanine's got black stockings rolled down. And fat bulges out around the roll. Then Nanine immerses her inflated arms in the bag and pushes and digs. Takes some kind of count. How she can tell anything that way I don't know. The bag's full. Deep. But Nanine burrows. Them fingers inch their way down. Wiggle, wiggle.

She plunges. And this was one of them few times she's bent over. Her head goes down. I look at her face. It's round and lumpy. Hard. Hard lumpy. And her hair's black. Indian black. With white strings that go from her forehead to where she's got it tied in back. Tied with a piece of the piping.

Now's when I breathe. The only time. While Nanine's inside the shopping bag. When she comes up I look down. I can hear her thick, heavy, suffocated chest sucking like a bellows. She uses her nubby pencil, got spit on it, to write some numbers or something in a very old notebook. The notebook got bent, brown and yellow stained edges.

Then Nanine's arms start to suck in stuff from all around her. I feel like too close to a boat in the ocean and I'm gonna get vacuumed in a whirlpool. She's got new, full spools of the material, with scraps of paper pinned to them with numbers on them. And then some samples of new things for mom to make.

"Aspetta, mia fanciulla, Marie." And she tugs and pulls at some poor little bow or loop, then forces it back together again. "Aspetta!" And mom gets in closer to see. I'm holding on to the back of mom's dress.

"Sì" mom says. It's the only time I hear her speak Italian except when we go to grandma's.

"Sì, Nanine." And mom's got another shopping bag she had

folded inside the one we brought. And she fills it up with the new stuff while Nanine's saying, "Buona fanciulla, Marie." Which I later find out means, "good girl, Mary." All the time I thought it was some kind of thank you. But Nanine don't say thank you. Mom does though. So do I. I'd always echo mom's thank you wherever we went. Thank you.

About here's where I was going to school. St. Mary's Gate of Heaven grammar school. And mom started going to work at Nanine's. Dad didn't like it. Only a half a day was all he'd agree to. Only half a day. So's I don't come home to an empty house, which mom don't want either. Dad must have been on day shift then. That happened a couple of times. Anyway, mom would beat me home no matter what.

I'd get out at five to twelve and walk home for lunch. We lived a half block from the school and the church for that matter. And mom would be there, standing up. She'd stand up all through lunch it seemed. But she sat down for a cup of coffee. Which is when I'd run back to the schoolyard. Run back to get in a game of slapball before the bell rang and all the kids in their blue pants and skirts, and white shirts and blouses, all tumbled into a line and marched inside.

But sometimes mom wasn't there. Dad was instead. One of his Monday or Tuesday days off. And he'd cook his 'amenda' omelet for me and him. A thick omelet with mint leaves from his garden. And he used the pan to flip it in the air. I never saw anybody else actually do that, except on tv.

"Your mother's at Nanine's, she'll be here any minute," he'd say looking over his shoulder and up at the wall clock while we finished the 'amenda' omelet. Then mom'd come hurrying in the skinny alleyway, the one the car don't go in. I'd pass her as I'm running out.

"Gotta go, mom, slapball, hi."

"Don't get hurt."

"No, bye." But on some days, when dad was at work, mom sometimes went back to Nanine's in the afternoon. I saw her a couple of times from my classroom window. She was walking on Jerome Avenue with the shopping bag. And it felt good to see her.

"Look, there's my mom." And other kids would jump up and crowd at the window.

Big deal?

But it was.

One time I remember going to Nanine's myself. By myself! I was old enough to cross streets. Was when mom was working at Nanine's. But where the people worked wasn't Nanine's room. Wasn't where Nanine sat. Was her house but a different part. The smell was there but less.

I get there and open a cheap plywood door. Stand in a curtained doorway. There are four rows of heavy-set women. All with their hair pulled back. And their arms so big. So round. Working. Those arms working, feeding material from bolts that lie in puddles all around the floor, feeding it into wide iron sewing machines. There's no ceiling lights, just individual goose neck lamp bulbs, one attached to each machine. The women keep forcing the cloth into the chattering machines. In the near dark. And there's dust. Cloth dust. I can hardly find mom. But she somehow knows I'm there and she stands up. The only one, from halfway down a row in the center. This ain't our parlor.

Draft Cards

About the time of the big one, WW Vietnam, I was just ripe for harvest. Aged to perfection. Pick me like a melon.

Up till now been keeping government hound dogs off my feet by being a college boy. Then I flunk out. Seems like the very next day I get a letter and a subway token. Letter says I got to go down to someplace street for a big physical. The token is saying, maybe I don't come back.

So the night before, with plenty of help from buddies in the neighborhood, I transform myself into a hopeless, disgusting drug mess.

"You wanna look and be your worse for the morning," friends say. And by the morning, I do. But just for some extra measure, after my coffee and toast, I shoot more dope and cocaine. Okay, now I'm ready to go on the Uncle Sam interview.

I get to the place, Whitehall Street or someplace like that. I don't remember how I got there, but I arrive. On time.

"Hupp-hup," take off my clothes.

"Hupp-hup," go sit on the bench.

"Hupp-hup," go sit on another bench. And hupp, I go here, and hupp, I go there. Thirteen hupps altogether, I think. Each one poke me, "hupp." And test me, "hupp." And write evaluations, "hupp-hupp-hupp." I'm failing miserably at everything. I notice the words "drug addiction" keeps showing up.

"Yupp."

Number thirteen is the psychiatrist. He's looking over all the twelve folders. Makes little scribbles in his folder. Then he looks up at me, "that's it," he says, and closes his folder.

"Now what?" I ask him.

"Go home," he tells me, "we don't want you."

I snap my feet together and salute him with a flat hand up on my eyebrow, "fine, I ain't too fond of you neither, bye."

I get a 2-S, or a 1-Y classification on my draft card, can't remember which. Either way it's a medical no-go. So I show up back at the local park.

"Hey, how you make out?" Chef-Boy-Arty asks me. "Where's your rifle?"

"No rifle," I say. "No knife, no bazooka, no machine gun, no tank, no airplane, no soldier suit." I got a smile on.

"Ho, how come?"

"I'm unclean, thank you. And they only want pearly whites shooting their guns and killing their enemies. So, fine."

What comes of this got nothing to do with the army. But it's got everything to do with draft cards. Was around this time draft cards were the number one form of identification. Like a passport in a foreign country. They get you into bars, dance places that got alcohol and age limits, stuff like that. If you're under age, a draft card is a valuable thing to get your hands on.

I get enlightened about this, big time, when one night, me and friend, Feather, go to buy dope in an uptown part of Manhattan. We park Feather's car nice and safe, walk the rest of the way. But when we come back, with good dope in our possession, no car.

Feather's hopping mad. Spittin out all kinds of, "fuckin shit, goddamn assholes, sonvabitch!" I notice a street sign, says, tow away zone. Uh oh, I think.

"Feather," I say, "look, at least we know where it is. Got towed, right?" Feather's looking at me like I just told him I ate it. I convinced Feather we should find out where they take towed cars. And we do. Way over on the west side. Feather wants to take a taxi, he's so pissed. I suggest we save our money and use a bus. We take a taxi. We get there.

"Yup," a shrunken little man in a shrunken little shack tells us, "we got that car. Cost you seventy-five bucks, plus thirty-five for the parking ticket," he grins at us. Feather's feet is twitching.

"How much you got?" I ask Feather. He don't bother to answer me. He just gives me a look which says he wants to go inside the shrunken little shack and kill the shrunken little man. Fact is, I know we don't have any money since we just spent what we had on dope, and a taxi ride. So we hang around the lot, looking through the hurricane fence at all the cars, trying to figure out what to do.

Real soon, two men come over to us. Look pretty normal. They say to us, "what you boys doing?"

"Trying to get our car back, but we got no money."

"Hey, boys your age must have draft cards," one of them says.

"Huh?" I say, looking over at Feather.

Feather says, "sure, so what," still pretty pissed, and not being very cordial like to the strangers.

"Well, maybe we know a way you boys can get your car outta the pound here."

"How's that," Feather's still cocky, but interested too.

"Maybe you might want to sell us your draft cards?"

"What, you wanna buy a draft card?" I ain't seeing the sense to this at all yet.

"That's right," one of them says, while the other one's nodding his head. And that's what happened. They give us sixty bucks each for our draft cards.

We spring Feather's car from the prison and we drive home, but all along the way my head gears are clicking. Here I am, going to art school, making with the T-square and learning how to set up mechanical art for printing presses and all that, and now I discover that some piece of junk card, which got no more fancy on it than anything I ever done on a drawing table, is worth some good piece of money.

"Ding, ding, ding!" I say to Feather, but he's only interested in crabbing about how creeps put their hands all over his car.

The next day, I'm in the draft card manufacturing business. "Hey, what classification you want? 1-A, 2-S, 4-F? You name it, you got it," I'm telling everybody. And I go on having a ball of fun. Make nice little draft cards and laminate them. Lamination makes it so you can't feel the texture of the card which is thinner than real cards. But they look pretty good. And I sell them like hotcakes. Use money to buy dope.

Then one day, sitting in the park, my friend Beegee comes up to me, says, "hey, two guys nose'n around here yesterday. Don't look like narc cops, but look real official like. Suit'n tie. Looking for somebody named Gregory." Beegee opens his eyes wide at me, like as if to say, that ring a bell?

I say, "Gregory who?"

Beegee says, "they don't know Gregory who, just know Gregory."

"Uh, oh, time to hang up my T-square and scram the neighborhood."

Beegee says, "hey, you got any dope?"

I get kind of panicky for the next few weeks. Positive it's J. Edgar Hoover himself on my trail. I start walking in back of trees. Hop in the bushes whenever an unfamiliar car goes by. Stay out of any one place for too long. Tell everybody, "start calling me Ralphie, no more Gregory."

I decide to have one big going out of business sale. Wind up unloading bulk draft cards to crazy Charlie Hillman. Crazy Charlie buys up what I got left at a great price. "Special, this week only," is what I told him. And I also think, good, maybe

Charlie'll start selling them and J. Edgar go looking for him instead of me.

But I ain't positive about this, so for extra precaution, me, Big Bell, Feather, and Chef-boy-Arty go up to the Canadian border, on a fishing trip. Something we been talking about doing for a while. Now's a good time, for me. We load up Feather's car with a couple of bags of clothes, and one big bag full of a healthy drug mix. Bring one fishing pole. A record player. And tons of records. Boys going fishing. Having fun.

Fishing Trip

Just want to talk about the fishing trip, then get on to more details about Big Bell and Feather. First though, I got to mention Chef-Boy-Arty.

Chef-Boy-Arty's quick to tell about. He got his name because his name is Arthur, and he likes to cook hamburgers and heat up cans of that Chef-Boy junk. Chef-Boy this, Chef-Boy that. Sometimes he eats it cold out of the can.

Before the fish trip he liked to drink Clan MacGregor whiskey and sit around out back of his house in an old truck trailer body. He had it like a clubhouse. It was surrounded with weeds. His mother was dead and him and his dad just didn't care a whole lot about things like weeds in the yard, or for that matter, getting rid of the decaying old tractor trailer.

Chef-Boy also entered into the fun world of drugs and liked to snort up speed drugs. Only he didn't get speedy from it. He usually just sat in the truck trailer with candles lit. And the weeds kept getting bigger.

After the fish trip, Chef-boy started taking excess amounts of cocaine and methadrine speed, a very strong, powerful, knock down elephant type of speed drug. He took so much, he went berserk, thinking cops were hiding in the ceiling of his house and under the truck. He didn't go out in the truck no more, and never went to sleep at night, just kept an eye on the ceiling.

Then one day he flushed all his methadrine and cocaine, tons of it, down the toilet. He boarded up his house windows and didn't come out for weeks. Never took drugs anymore. Then he disappeared altogether. I didn't see him till years and years later when he shows up working in a truck supply store, looking kind of still and docile. Oh well, least he's alive.

Okay, so we drive north on the New York State Thruway, aim Feather's car at Canada. Fish be real happy if all fishermen are like us. We settle in a place called Ogdensburg because the name sounds good. Friendly. Not likely to have FBI agents there.

We get a cabin, old wood and leaning to the left, right on the river. And we get a motor boat. We got one fish pole, a net, a container of worms, which Chef-Boy-Arty keeps playing with, holding up worms by the tail, telling us, "this is the tail, this is the head, know how I can tell?" But nobody cares how he can tell, or which side the worm's head is on.

And we got a few gallons of wine, some cans of beer, a shopping bag filled to the top with pot, a plastic baggie filled with hallucinogenic drugs, a big flat wad of tin foil with cocaine and methadrine, and dope. Heroin. Going fishing.

First few days we don't get beyond the cabin porch. We can't figure how to get this fish thing off the ground. We sit in the big old broken easy chairs and talk about getting going. We set up the record player, and keep it going steady. Kids in the area come around after a while, friendly like. They watch us. Listen to us. Laugh at us. We laugh back. We play Rolling Stones music over and over. Tell the kids that it's us. We're the Rolling Stones.

"Yeah, that's us," Big Bell says. And he tells them he's Charlie Watts, since he's got drumsticks which he uses all the time to disperse some kind of equal amount of metabolism that his huge body is activated at. Big Bell must be almost four-hundred pounds, about six feet tall. With a voice that's buried way down deep inside all his fat. And Bell can't play no drums, he

just makes nervous action taps here and there, and on everything. Sometimes he plays on Chef-Boy-Arty's head, which
Chef-Boy don't like.

But the river kids, they look at us confused, so we keep
insisting it's us, the Rolling Stones, and we play more records
and sing along, "see . . ." They half believe us. They're pretty
young. They figure we must be something, after all, they never
seen nothing like us, so we must be something.

On the third day we march out to the boat. Takes us hours
to get the boat launched, keep running back to the cabin
because somebody forgot something. And sometimes we forget
altogether why we're back in the cabin. We finally get out in the
boat. Row out a ways before we start the engine.

"Gimme, lemme do it."

"Gimme, lemme do it."

"Gimme, lemme do it."

"You guys don't know whatcha doin, gimme, lemme do it."
We drift all the way down the river, into a piece of land sticking way out. Good thing. We take advantage of the land while
we got it, use the oars to gondola ourselves on shore. Get out,
walk back to the cabin. Enough fishing for today.

We pay the kids to go get the boat for us. Bring it back,
show us how to work the motor. Rolling Stones ain't too good
with engine trouble. While they are at it, local kids show us a
funny thing they do with fish once they catch them. Kids run a
hundred foot electric cord down to the dock. Get themselves an
electric kitchen knife, and a blender.

"Rrrrrpp," off goes the fish head.

"Rrrrrpp," off goes his tail. Then up one side the fish and
down the other. "Rrrrrpp." Throw what they got in the blender.
Couple of quick high speed spins in the blender, take it out, and
pat-pat, they got pike burgers. Or any kind of fish they catch,
burgers. This don't seem natural to us, but hey, they live here.

So, anyway, next day we try it again. We get the hang of it.

Till we run the boat onto a sandbar, break a propeller blade. Next day, new propeller, try it again. Now Feather's not interested no more, stays in the cabin. Me, Chef-Boy-Arty and Big Bell go out.

"This looks like a good spot, toss over the anchor." Rope feeds out quick after Bell gives the anchor a heave, like it was a shot put. Rope keeps feeding out, right over the side and sinks with the anchor.

"You forgot to tie the end of the rope to the boat, dummy."

"Who's a dummy?"

"You's a dummy, dummy."

We can't fish too good drifting, current's too fast. Motor boat back to the cabin. Now Chef-Boy's losing interest. Don't want to go in the boat no more. Me neither, too much pain in the neck. But Big Bell wants to go for a ride.

So Bell goes back out alone, with a cinder block tied to a new rope for a new anchor. Bell's so big, he weighs down the back of the boat where he's got to sit with one hand on the engine throttle. He weighs it down so much that the front end of the boat sticks way up high in the water. Off goes Bell, boat sticking up at maybe a sixty-degree angle.

A lot of time goes by Bell don't come back. Late day sunset looks pretty good, so we go sit down on the dock, wait for Bell to come in. Then we see a little speck on the water, coming closer.

"Looks like Bell."

"Yup, it's Bell. Here comes Bell."

"Rrrrrrrrrrrr," there goes Bell, right past us. Bell missed the cabin. Kept going. A little while later, same thing happens, from the other direction.

"Here come Bell."

"Yup, that's Bell."

"There goes Bell."

Bell went right by again. We agree this is like watching a

cartoon show. Finally, Big Bell spots the cabin, and us. Turns in toward the dock.

"Here comes Bell."

"Yup, that's Bell."

"Bell better slow down."

"Yup, better slow down."

But Bell don't slow down. Crashes right into the dock. We all jump and run. Pieces of dock fly in all directions. Big Bell flips over backwards, splashes in the water. If Bell had a flipper he'd look like one of them whales doing a dive like they do. But Bell don't have no flipper. He's out in the water, arms flapping and he's hollering. Everybody's mad at Bell now, since he lost our fish pole, and some drugs and a gallon of wine, and he broke the dock, which we got to fix. Which we do, till we use up the rest of our drug groceries, then, time to go home.

Feather

Feather's a good looking guy. Girls bend over backwards to be with Feather. And Feather knows that plenty. Feather's always got a cat grin. Always ready for a good deal. All the time he's got that cocky strut. Even when he's doped. Feather's so cocky he sells drugs from his car trunk like hot dogs. Just pulls up to the local park, opens trunk, says, "okay, store's open."

One time, Feather, me, and Big Bell, we're traveling up Harlem to get some dope. Feather's got convertible top down. Nice day. I'm in the front with Feather. Big Bell in the back. Big Bell got to go in the back. He's so big, he don't fit in the front.

We comin up on an open fire hydrant. Hot day. Kids cooling off in the gutter with fire sprinkle. Kids playing, hold something over the open water spout, make a long spray. Lotsa water.

Feather says, "better put the top up."

Bell says, "that's smart, Feather." Bell and Feather get along okay but alla time antagonize each other back and forth. Both of 'em got a lot of sarcasm. Feather's comes from cocky. Bell's comes from big. Bell very big. Draft card says, OBESE. No letters, no numbers.

Feather stops his car. Motors the top up. Okay. Feather steps on the gas, hard. Figures he'll get through the water splash fast that way. But the splash completely covers the windshield.

Feather's blinded by the water, but his foot's not paying much attention. It don't hear the message, can't see, and it stays down on the pedal.

Boop! And I'm on Feather's hood. Praying all the wet ain't my blood. Turns out, half and half. Some fire hydrant water, but my face's all cut and leaking blood, too. Feather hits two parked cars, all innocent and bystanding. Lotta black people come around, yelling at us, like, "you white, what you doing here anyway?"

Me, I say, "hey, how about some human kindness. I'm hurt." But their cars hurt too, and that's important to them. Turns out, Big Bell's hurt too. Got some metal sticking out his leg. Feather, he tries to calm everybody down before they beat up his car. Lotsa scuffle going on.

I got my head in the cold hydrant water now. Spoiling kids' fun by bleeding on the cool-off water. Then a big lady comes over, black lady, puts a big black hand under my chin, tip up-like. Got other big hand on my neck, presses firm. She marches me to corner drug store, tells the drug store man, "need some cotton and peroxide for the boy here."

The big lady says to me, "you got money boy?" I fish in my pocket and pull up something. Give it over. She lets go of my head, gives money to the drug store man, then her big fat hand stuffs change back in my pocket. Next, she wads me up, all puffy and antiseptic, and leads me back to the scene of the accident. It's plenty hostile now. Good thing Big Bell's with us. He gets out of the car, and lotsa people go the other way. This is good, but also feeds into Feather's cockyness.

Feather starts struttin, saying, "these mothers think we pussy." And, "hey, lookit my windshield!"

Bell says, "fuck you, Feather, you make your car get outta here or I'll break all the little parts in your head." Bell's got his meaty hand flat down on his leg. Not much blood there, but a funny piece of metal sticking out a few inches between Bell's fat fingers. Bell's not in a big hurry to admit this but I think he's hurt and don't fancy no fight right now.

I'm gurgling now, throat all bloody, and my head hurts. "Feather, let's get out of here." Feather's still acting cocky but no dummy.

"Okay," he says, "but we coulda handled 'em."

Bell says, "Feather, you don't go now I make you not so good lookin." This the kind of talk that wiggles its way to the part of Feather's brain that makes him move. Inna car we go. Brruup, brrruup!

I'm needing dope now lots more than before. I say, "get to connection now, please, hurry." I'm wondering at the same time, where that big lady come from, or go to. I'm thinking, she was nice, first time black hand do doctor work on me.

Now, if Big Bell was still alive, and God knows where Feather is, maybe they'd fill you in on the missing parts here. But Bell's dead now, and Feather? Who knows?

So I skip now to . . . arrive back at the park. Home.

All the park folk saying, "lookit you. What happened? Lookit'cha face. Your nose."

I say, "no problem, I'm okay, got plenty heroin in me. Everything's okay."

Feather's puffing around saying, "my windshield ain't so good."

Bell's over on the park bench, pouring what's left of peroxide on his leg. Got a four inch piece of metal spring from the back of Feather's car seat in his hand. He's yelling at Feather, "Feather, this yours, I oughtta sue you."

Feather says, "sue me, fatso." But he says this not for Bell to hear. He knows better.

Dead-Phily comes up to me and snugs my nose between his palms. He's looking me in the eye, saying, "that's broke for sure." Then he goes snap-a-roo. And he says, "there, that's better." It sounds to me like a pencil snap. Feels like somebody tap me on back of the head. Don't really hurt though. Heroin's number one pain killer.

Girlfriend, Antoinette, mad at me taking so long bringing home dope, till she sees my face, all crooked nose and purple eyes, and bloody, bloody shirt. Then she's only half mad.

"You get the dope?" she says.

Antoinette

One thing special about Antoinette, her mom sews clothes.
Antoinette got home clothes. Interesting. But what's real special
about Antoinette, her whole face smiles. Not a spot left
unhappy when Antoinette smiles. And she does it in slow
motion-like. So smile lasts a long time.

Antoinette and me, we're partners. Boyfriend, girlfriend,
but partners too. Partners in the dope chase. It don't start out
that way but it ends up that way. Starts out boy meets girl, girl
meets boy.

In natural evolution of the neighborhood, boy and girl get
high together. Goes along with smoochy-smooch, holding hands
and going to the movies. In natural evolution of getting high,
boy and girl climb ladder of get-high drugs. Same old story
about one thing leading to two things. No sense wasting a lotta
breath on one-thing, two-thing detail. We get to heroin. And
likewise, heroin gets to us. Full time work.

Spend most our time running round looking for money.
Running round looking for needles. Running round looking
for heroin. And running round looking for dark place to make
heroin, needle and us, sing. And Antoinette sings extra with
her smile.

Good work to have a partner in, although dope partners
got a reputation for not being so reliable. Not always, not one

hundred percent. No such thing in heroin work. Still, a partner's a partner. And a girlfriend's a girlfriend. (Boyfriend's a boyfriend too, I hope, to Antoinette).

A particular good thing about having a dope partner is, when you get sick and got no dope, sick feels less sick split in half. Two moan together better than one moaning alone. Antoinette and me, we moan good together when we got no dope. Harmony like. But harmony just for dope moaning, not sex moaning. Body's all too fruitcake for that. Body's all inside and out. Everything hurts when dope sickness comes on. You just feel clammy, sweaty, pukey, moany, twitchy, hammer-head like, bamboo shoot under fingernail, watermelon up the ass, sick. Not a good time for sex.

First time Antoinette and me got together sex-like, I don't remember. Second time, I remember. And it wasn't fun. Up on some old abandoned railroad tracks. Cement platform, glass bottles alla round. No clothes. Antoinette looked so good. Antoinette felt so warm. But the glass was a nuisance. Drugs don't help. Drug famous for penis shrinkle. Drug also got a sense of humor. Drug tells head, "go ahead, you can do it, feels good."

So head tells shrinkle penis, "c'mon, get going, you missing out on the fun." But drug already let all the air outta penis, and that's that.

What does Antoinette think? I wonder if she's got any compare-like problem? Maybe she's thinking, oh well, don't care, got a boyfriend, nice boy, means well, sex ain't everything. But who knows? Anyway it feels good to be close and that what's important.

Eventually we get this sex thing worked out, pretty much. Sex is like putting together Japanese toys. Comes out better when you just pay attention, don't follow step by step instruction. But old heroin a pretty strong drug and makes things all mixed up. Sometimes we ask each other, did we do it?

"I dunno."

"You in there?"

"Think so, you feel me in there?"

"That you?"

Later, Antoinette's first abortion proves to us both that somebody in there. This a sad time. Friend Marie goes with Antoinette to the abortion place. I go buy dope. Antoinette not too nice to me for a while. I try to understand, but I'm not a girl. Do what a boy can do. Hold hand, soothe ruffled feathers, pat tummy, hug and hold, buy chocolate, buy dope, never, never mention word baby. Time helps heal, for me. Time like a leaky band-aid for Antoinette. But she's strong. Pulls up bootstraps, and gets on with life business.

One way we sleep together, Antoinette sneaks up to my bedroom. Goes past the hall between kitchen and mom and dad's bedroom. Antoinette walks shoulder to me and we scoot by, like one person. One time, mom says from the bedroom, "Gregory, that somebody with you?"

"Naw, just a shadow. G'night." And we creak, creak quiet as we can all night long. Then, in the morning, Antoinette got to sneak out, hippity-hop-like. It usually goes something like this: Mom's at the kitchen with coffee, Antoinette's down the stairs, ducks under dining room table. Mom goes up in sewing room to get something, Antoinette zips down to the cellar. Mom goes in the bathroom, Antoinette out the cellar door. Dad's already at work. Antoinette's parents think she's at a girl-friend's house.

Another day gets going, gotta get some money to get some dope. We do crazy things for money. We steal anything sits still more'n two minutes. Sometimes less. We steal dopey things nobody gives us hardly anything for. Dad's old electric razor, Antionette's mom's not so hot jewelry. Try to hock 'em. Try to sell 'em.

Then we learn, better off going straight for money. Steal

coin collections. Steal from parents' pockets. Steal store cash boxes. Steal liquor too, that change to money quick. Once, I'm caught one leg in and one leg out, cousin Frankie's next door, bedroom window. Going for Uncle Carmine's liquor. Got good stuff. Expensive stuff. Uncle Joe, on other side of Frankie's, come around backyard and says, "hey, what are you doing?"

I say, "looking for Frankie," and I keep going in the window. Frankie's family's out that time of day. Antionette sees what's happening and runs in quick, asking Uncle Joe lotsa dumb questions, makes him turn around. Who knows what Uncle Joe thinks at the time? Who cares? I get the liquor. Sell it to gas station guy few blocks away. Go buy dope with liquor money.

One time, Antoinette and me, we're sick. Need dope bad.

"Oh woe, what we gonna do?" Antoinette says.

"We gonna die, that's what, Antoinette," I say. We kick street trash, huddled up close, walking like one person with four legs. Cold out. Antoinette kicks a paper bag. Money spills out. "Hey!" We jump onna money. Jump like crazy game show contestant. Forty-six dollars. Just like that, in a paper bag. "Wow, wee, wow!" We take nice warm taxi cab to seedy part of Brooklyn. We buy dope. We shoot dope. We're not sick no more, not cold no more.

One time, we cook up a big plan. We think it's big. Really it's dumb. Plan goes: I sit inna car, Antoinette goes in connection house.

Antoinette says to connection, "gimme fifteen bags please." Soon as Antoinette gets hands on the bags, she runs out of the house, into nice ready car. Then I step on the gas pedal. Good plan.

Turns out, it works. It's too dumb not to work. Oh, we hopping up and down, laughing. Antoinette's smile goes all way round her head. Only trouble with this plan, we realize later, we can't go back to that connection no more. Oh well.

69

Another time, another plan. We get a gun. A real gun. Like bangitty bang bullets and everything. I set up deal with new connection. Tell 'em I got a sappy young white girl with lots of sappy friends who got money to but lots of dope. Wants dope up front so she can sell it, come back and buy more. (Antoinette acts like sappy white chick). I let connection see gun, like as if by accident. Make this look like serious business. Antoinette acting like annoyed, like, let's get this over with, huh. She's doing such a good job. It's hard for me not to say, hey, Antoinette, that's pretty good. Instead, I act nervous like. I act like this gun might go off any second, and if this deal don't happen now, like quick, then I'll take sappy girl to some other connection.

Connection eyes us up, shrewd. Connection respects a gun and big money possibilities. He's pretty big time and don't get tricked too easy though. Says, "how we know you got the bucks?"

This the best part of the plan. I say, "hey, I carry this to blow my nose," and I dig in my pants pocket and pull up a wad of (what look like) big bills. I do this fast-like, as if big wad gonna burst into flames if it stay in the open air too long.

"See," I sez, and shove wad back in my pocket.

What this wad really is, is a bunch of fake stuff. Antoinette and me, we spend whole night doing paste-up and mechanical reproductions of Ben Franklins. They're really terrible but with the help of the fast glance and gun, they're good enough. Fast glance not as important as gun though. Gun got a funny ability to make things around it extra real.

Connection says, "how much you want?"

Antoinette says, "how much you got?"

I'm thinking, nice touch, Antoinette. There's a long pause now. Connection's eyeing us up and down some more.

"We ain't got all day," I say, pushing the thing along.

Connection says, "I give you two loads. You sell it, bring

back money, I give you four loads more. You keep selling I keep giving."

This is exactly what we hope connection'd do. We young punks push connection pride hard enough, connection gotta act bigger than us. Act bigger by taking investment chance. This connection's big time enough to do that once in a while.

Hey, we're dope fiends but not altogether dopey. We walk out calm and cool-like, two loads in the pocket, big fake wad in the other pocket. Gun stuck in my pants. We're in the dealing business. We make a lotta money. We make enough to pay off big connection and still have dope left over for us. But this don't last too long. We go back to big connection, give over the money, say, "see," and ask for bigger bunch, like promised. We get bigger bunch. Same deal, sell it, bring back money, get more. But being junkies, we screw up a good thing.

Junkies got this terrible habit of not looking too far in the future. And when they do, they say, worry about that later, gotta take care of now, now. Me and Antoinette shoot up almost all the big connection dope. Now we got no dope to sell and no money for the big connection. But it sure was good while it lasted.

"Now what we gonna do?" Antoinette and me ask each other. Big connection big enough to have us killed, and not miss lunch. For a week or two, we duck and hide. Word's out, we're dead meat. Then a lucky thing happens, big connection's house gets raided. Presto, magic, big connection in jail.

"Whew!" say Antoinette, "safe."

"Whew!" I say, "we're safe, but sick. What we gonna do?" That's the way dope chase goes. Hardly any time between good and bad. That time, the police do us a favor. But most the time, police a nagging nemesis. We always looking over our shoulders and moving in dark places. Hiding what we got, and hiding what we trying to get. Run and hide. Run and hide.

The Terribles

Time we're driving on Atlantic Avenue, Antoinette, me, Dead-
Phily and Danny Torelli. Just come back from the connection.
Just finish shooting dope. All of us sleepy. Nod. Dope nod.
Drive along nice and easy. On the way to famous diner, going
for tea and English muffins. All of a sudden, two cars zip up
along side us. One on the left, one on the right. They point guns
at us. Bull horn sounds like God, telling us, "STOP CAR, THIS
THE POLICE." Everybody wakes up, fast.

"Whoa," I say to the car.

Antoinette says, "whoa," too.

Dead-Phily says, "what the fuck?" Danny don't say anything, but his eyes, their spinning all round, and he sitting up in
the seat, ready. Danny's usually like that. Danny's short, fast.
Strong for little guy. Ready.

Two cop cars, disguised like regular cars, with lots of disguised cops inside looking like college kids in a telephone
booth. They make us stop with their guns and their cars. They
make us stop right where we're driving. They don't tell us to
pull over. They just say, STOP. Right in the middle of the three
lane avenue.

They pull us all out of the car. Legs spread, hands on hood.
Pull apart car, yank out seats right in the middle of traffic. Turn
us around, one at a time, look at arms for needle marks. We got

plenty. They start smacking inside and outside our legs. Turn pockets inside out, search us up and down.

Danny and Dead-Phily already used all their dope, they're clean. Danny starts getting arrogant. Cop comes up fast with a billy club between Danny's legs. Danny's got nothing else to say. Dead-Phily's too stoned to care about anything. He lets them shove and poke him round, like he's some kind of Raggedy Andy doll.

Cops make Antoinette unsnap bra, squeeze her arms together and shake. Good fortune smiling, Antoinette's got nothing hid in her bra. She got dope in her underpants, but cops a little reluctant-like to go hunting in there. Least not on Atlantic Avenue.

Cops not so reluctant with me. Cop puts his hand right down my pants and feels around. He hits the eyedropper tip and needle, all tied up with a rubber band. But he pulls his hand out and says, "okay, clean." Maybe he thinks he hit something else, and don't want to look queer? Clean? I think. Me, clean? You wrong mister cop, but if that's what you think, it's okay by me.

Cops say, "gwan, beat it ya creeps. See ya another time." They're smiling. We're all disoriented-like, but very happy not to be busted. Cops drive away, leave us with the inside of car all on the outside. We're blocking traffic. Lotsa honking going on. We hurry now, try to get car back together. In such a tizzy though, we leave the back seat out on the avenue. Gotta make a stupid U-turn and go back for it. Cars all swerve around it. We pull up behind it. Everybody starts honking again. Me and Danny get out, fast, open the back door, toss it in on top of Dead-Phily. He don't seem to mind. And we drive on to the diner.

Once in the diner, we calm down some. We all slide into a booth. Then we start to laugh. Nervous relief laugh. Kinda laugh you make when in school, you're cheating up a storm and the teacher hesitates by your desk, then moves on. You see teacher's tail lights moving down the aisle, and you go whew, and you laugh to yourself. We're all in the booth now, hissing and laughing. English muffins, with extra butter. Milky tea and lots of sugar all around.

But, another time, we get a surprise. Just me and Antoinette, coming outta connection house on 125th Street and Amsterdam Avenue. Uptown, Harlem. What are two white kids doing here? Unfortunately, cops know just what two white kids are doing here.

Cops roust us, then take us to the precinct house. Now the surprise. They got a lady cop. And, of course, regular men cops. Me and Antoinette gotta strip. Oh boy, they got us now. And they do. For Antoinette, it's the Girl's House of Detention. For me, it's down to Schermerhorn Street. Down in a dungeon cell. Ugly, dirty cell. Not nice.

Later, Antoinette comes out with horror story about girls, big scary girls, with broom handles and things, try to get friendly-like with her. But she acts loony, which Antoinette's pretty good at doing, and so they don't hurt her too much.

Back in Schermerhorn dungeon. Terrible cell with terrible men. Cell, regular dungeon size. Got fourteen terrible men, and me. One terrible, just lay in middle of the cell, got pants half down. Scratching and clawing at himself. Must have crabs, maybe lobsters the way he scratching. Nobody pays attention to him. Everybody looking at me. Got eyes for young boy's behind. This is dangerous. This a part of my body for things to come out, not go in. How am I gonna explain this to them? They start to worm around. Shape half moon around me. I got my back to cell wall, saying, "I'm a good boy, God, how bout you make me invisible, please?"

Now, this ain't too funny. These guys look like they don't got much to lose. I think about Antoinette. Hope she got no terribles on her. But I think about me now, more important. Big ugly one, pulling on my sleeve now, saying, "take your clothes off nice boy." I wonder, how's he know I'm a nice boy? Maybe if I don't act so nice, he'd lose interest? I act not nice. I yank back my sleeve and kick a foot out. But, oh boy, this has the opposite effect of what I want. He grabs my foot and pulls me on the floor. More moving in. Feel like a cooked goose now. Roast turkey. And they gonna eat me, giblets and all.

Then I hear, "Gregory, that you Gregory?" I look over to the cell gate. It's Milo. Milo in a cop coat, outside the cell. Milo turned good boy a few years back, became a court officer. Looks just like a cop, with cop outfit, hat even.

I say, "Oh Milo, you get me outta here and I'm lighting a candle in church for you."

Milo says "sit tight, be right back."

I say "just a second, Milo, I don't get a sit tight coming to me. Looks like old Mr. Terrible here is in a hurry." But Milo's gone in a whoosh. Now all terrible's eyes on me. This looks bad. How come a nice boy in the cell, friendly-like with cop outside the cell? They're asking, with gunpowder in their faces. I must be a rat person, they figure. And they know what to do with rat people. This ain't working out right at all. I think, Milo, you don't hurry back, there'll be lots of little Gregory all around the cell.

But praise, praise, Milo comes back. With a big fat, iron key. Milo's key has effect on terribles like Christ's cross on vampires. Clink, clunk, big iron door opens. Long cop arm reaches in, fishes around, snatches hold of me, and plunks me out, like a bear swattin fish out of the river.

"Whew." Good thing long arm of cop long enough. I get put in a private cell, right across the way from terribles. Only four or five feet away, but good enough. Big iron bars say that. Big old terribles not so big now. "Nyah, nyah," I say, real low like. Wish Antoinette was here now, we'd hop up and down together. Go, "nyah, nyah," together, and laugh. But I'm alone. That's good and that's bad.

Later, judge says, "This young boy is not a real criminal."

Just a drug boy. Judge gives me another chance. "Be good, or else," he says from inside what looks like a graduation gown.

"Yessir, yessir, three bags full," I say.

Outside, Antoinette and me pick up where we left off. She tells me about her terribles, and I tell her about mine. We both agree, best thing to do in future is don't go back to jail no how. Grab cop gun and shoot, if necessary. But it don't work out that way. We get picked up again in no time. Antoinette got nothing on her, shot it all up already. But I got dope in me, and on me, unfortunately. Antoinette goes home. I go to jail. Same old story.

Meet another drug friend in the cell. We two. That's better than one. We sit, sleep, stand and piss, back to back. See full circle that way. Got four feet and four fists to kick and punch with. Keep ourselves at a distance. For a while anyway. Long enough, thank goodness.

Family comes with bail money. I'm never happier to see them than now. I go before judge again. Different judge, same graduation suit. Same story, except for slight change in script. This judge says, "This boy's getting worse. He needs help. We want this boy in a drug rehabilitation."

"Yessir, yessir, yessir. I'm on my way already. G'bye."

I gotta go to a drug rehabilitation center, nine-to-five, in Brooklyn. Every day, for a month. After that I'm supposed to be evaluated for whether or not I need more rehabilitation, maybe have to go into a live-in program, no more nine-to-five. Or maybe they say I'm hopeless and need to go back to jail. Or maybe they say success case and send me home. I'm counting on home.

Drug rehabilitation place ain't too bad. I go every morning and spend all day. Got a lot of declawed terribles in it. And some kids like me. And some just starting out, like used-to-be-me.

I tell Antoinette, "got to go, or else back to jail."

She says, "this is better. Not too bad, we'll see each other at night."

This cuts into our dope time, but we make do. One good thing, at least I'm cleaned up a little. Leave most of my habit in the jail cell, and ain't doing nearly as much now since I spend all day in rehab. But build habit right back up pretty quick. It's easy. Antoinette still got her habit all along. She needs dope maybe two, three times a day. She usually meets me at five, when I get out. She's sometimes sick, sometimes got dope. Sometimes she tells me what she got to do to get dope during the day, sometimes not. At night we go get dope together. I pretend to family that I'm doing good though. They want to believe this, real bad, so they do. Funny thing about lying. When you lie in somebody's face, ain't much they can do. Either they say, you lying, or they say, okay I believe you. In this case, until more evidence comes in, family says, okay, we believe.

Partnership with Antoinette's under some stress now. It's hard for one person to do dope chase when the other person is only working half time. This nine-to-five rehabilitation is interfering with business. We need to beef up our work force. And that's when we start taking up with Gilbert.

Gilbert

Gilbert's some funny character. Older than us. Older junkie. Gilbert's been shootin dope, fifteen, twenty years. But he's still got silly in him. Gilbert's small. Small fingers, small body, small face. Wears real old-fashioned glasses. Little kid type glasses. Got permanent Scotch tape on one of the hinges. Turned yellow, like his eyes. He's got nervous eyes. He's got nervous everything. Fidgets all the time. Talks fast, walks fast, and waves his arms around a lot. Makes you crazy being around him too long. But, as annoying as Gilbert can get, he's still a top notch dope fiend. Always manages to come up with something. Got to. Since he's already down to bare bones, there's no room for failure.

"Whatever it takes," is what Gilbert always says. Deviation, flimflam and audacity (Gilbert's words) is what usually works. Course, sometimes he lands in jail too, and he's gone for a while. But sooner or later, he always manages to get out again. And soon as he gets out, "it's straight to the cooker," as he's fond of saying.

I think going to jail now and then's all that keeps Gilbert alive. Jail gives him a chance to kick his habit, bring down his tolerance some, so he don't need so much dope to get high when he gets out (not that there's no dope in jail) and generally, get back in shape for grueling heroin work.

Gilbert's got a wife, named Janie, and two kids. Little Gilberts (I hope not). Wife, Janie, shoots dope once in a while, but tries hard to maintain something that looks like dignity. Tries to keep a household. Not easy to do with Gilbert coming and going. Kids sometimes dirty, sometimes clean.

Janie's usually glad when Gilbert's home, but she's gotta nail down everything, including kids' milk money. For that matter, kids too. Janie usually manages this, she's big. I think she even beats Gilbert up now and then.

I know she beat him silly one time, after she came home from the store and found no door where the house front door used to be. Gilbert sold the door! Needed dope money. Nice heavy wooden door. One time she came home just in time to catch Gilbert with the kitchen stove halfway down the steps. Gilbert got a black eye from Janie on that one. Too bad somebody can't harness all Gilbert's energy, probably come up with some kind of fuel. Enough to power electric appliances maybe.

Up till now, me and Antoinette smart enough to stay away from Gilbert. Everybody knows not to trust him. He'd steal your pants and sell 'em back to you, if you're not careful. But we getting pressed lately. Not generating enough dope-cash flow, with me in the drug rehab all day, and Antoinette wearing herself out hustling alone.

So we take up with Gilbert. Leastways, Antoinette goes and joins him up in the partnership. First time I realize this is when Antoinette shows up to meet me outside the rehab, and she's got Gilbert with her. She tells me Gilbert got a sure-fire plan. Both of 'em already doped.

Gilbert jumps right in, says, "hey, Gregorio, my boy, c'mon, we go get you a taste, how's that sound?" Gilbert the only person in the world that calls me by my Italian name, except for maybe my grandparents.

I say, "you got it on you?"

Gilbert says, "what do I look like? C'mon, we go get it."

For a couple of seconds, I'm thinking, Gilbert's dangerous to be with. 'Specially when he's doped. Takes crazy chances. But worse when he's sick. Gilbert'll do absolutely anything then. So I figure, guess now's the best bet. Besides, I'm coming down with light sniffling. (Sure sign of dope sickness coming on).

"Where to," I say. Antoinette smiles, big, soft, sleepy dope smile. Us three walk at Gilbert's pace. Fast, choppy steps. Steadily tipping to the right. I gotta do a hop-skip every three steps to keep in sync. Then all of us bump back to the left. And start over again. Gilbert walks unnatural.

Gilbert says, "Sonny, over on Avenue A, he owes me. We go to Sonny's house first, get you straight, Gregorio, my man." Sure enough, Sonny gives Gilbert six bags. Gilbert gives me two, one to Antoinette, she's already got some in her, and he keeps three bags for himself.

I shoot up the two bags. Immediately cure the sniffles. Like it cures lumbago, diarrhea, heartbreak of psoriasis, herpes (makes you forget you got 'em anyway) backache, frontache, sideache, and anything else that aches or makes you uncomfortable. For all its bad sides, heroin's sure a wonder drug.

Now I'm feeling like, this Gilbert jazz, good idea on Antoinette's part. Till I find out later that Gilbert pimps off Antoinette to Sonny, that's why Sonny owes Gilbert dope. Shit! But that's part of junkie world. Big part.

It becomes part of dope chase for me and Antoinette on other occasions too. Sometimes, we got no money, and we're sick, and Antoinette goes into connection house, comes out with dope for me and for her. It's something we don't talk about. Just accept. Although, to tell the truth, I'm never thrilled to death about it. And I always wonder, does Antoinette like it? Or does Antoinette hate it? She don't act like she hates it. She don't act like it even ever happens. Nothing happening, 'cept getting and shooting dope.

We're all straight now. Got dope sickness monster sucking

on lollipops. Now it's time to hear Gilbert's plan. Plan requires us to first break into a uniform rental shop on Flatbush Avenue. After hours. The place's long since closed. No tight security, not a lot of people steal uniforms. We break into a back window. Smash it up. I climb inside, open up the side door for Gilbert and Antoinette. We pick out two workmen pair of coveralls. One for me and one for Gilbert. Antoinette scavenges around for anything else that looks valuable. Not much. Now we got uniforms. "Now what?" I say.

Gilbert says, "these for tomorrow morning, don't worry, this works out good, I promise."

"Ho, lotta good promise from Gilbert's worth," I say to Antoinette. Antoinette laughs. Gilbert laughs too.

We go back to Gilberts' house for the night. Strange there. Family and all. Wife, Janie, acts nice to us, but looks miserable herself. Kids playful but filthy. This is not one of Janie's better days. Place pretty filthy too. Janie's drunk.

Janie says, "wanna smoke some pot?" We do that. Not a good idea though. Brings on end of dope faster. We're restless, toss'n turn'n the night away. In the morning, Gilbert lets Antoinette and me split up one of his bags, just enough to ward off dope sickness. Gilbert sucks up the other two bags. Janie drinking coffee.

Now we dress up in the uniforms. Mine says, Ray, on the pocket. Gilbert's says, Frankie. Antoinette calls us Frankie and Ray all day. We take a subway to Brooklyn business district.

Gilbert says, "be onna lookout for a plain looking van, something not fancy." We get off train before the business district to look. We find a panel truck parked on Myrtle Avenue. I break open the back door, easy like. Gilbert wires ignition, quick. And we drive off. Bump, bump. I'm driving. Gilbert in the passenger seat. Antoinette sits on the thing in the middle. We go to Board of Health Department building. Antoinette stays in the truck, keeps it running, and also keeps ticket maid from calling tow truck. She acts like she's waiting for a delivery. In a way, it's true. Me and Gilbert (Frankie and Ray) go walking into big office pool. Zillions of secretaries, all clickity, click at their typewriters.

Gilbert says, "do like me."

I say, "I do like you, I be dead tomorrow." Gilbert gives me a shut up look. Gilbert looks funny with work suit on, and Scotch tape glasses.

We walk up to a secretary way in the back. Gilbert says, "this the one?" And he tilts up the typewriter that the secretary's working on, right while she's typing. He says to her, 'scuse me." And he looks at the serial numbers on the bottom. Then he says, "yup, this the one, right?" to me.

I say, "yeah, that's the one all right," while I'm looking at a piece of paper with a silly poem on it for Antoinette. Pretend it's got the same serial numbers on it.

Gilbert says, "scuse me," again, and he goes around to her side of the desk, and bends down by her legs, following the electric cord. Secretary backs away on rolling chair, in a hurry. Gilbert unplugs the typewriter, lifts it up, and off we go. Secretary just sitting there, in front of an empty desk. Confusion fills up the space where the typewriter used to be. Nobody else even looks up. We scoot down the length of the office pool.

Out the door we go, back in the truck. Antoinette got laugh all over her. Smacking her head with her palm, saying, "I don't believe it."

"Believe it," says Gilbert. "And there's more where that come from."

We do this all morning. Different buildings, different typewriters. Sometimes, the same building, but a different floor or office. By lunchtime, we got a dozen nice typewriters. We take 'em to a fence Gilbert's familiar with in the area. The fence gives us a hundred bucks each for six of 'em. And fifty for the other six. We still got the truck we stole. Might as well drive to the connection house, we all agree. We buy dope. We shoot dope. Gotta say though, Gilbert's not a pleasant sight to watch shooting dope. He's been at it so long, he's got permanent holes in his arms. He don't need to break the skin anymore, just slide the needle in one of his mucous like openings.

In the Post Office

Once, I got a job working in the United States Post Office, on
34th Street and 8th Avenue. I work the four to midnight shift.
Work in the lower level, the basement, where packages, boxes,
magazines and things go through. No letters.

I work at a conveyor belt. Stand in one spot while boxes,
boxes, and more boxes go by. This is the "seconds" belt. Where
packages that already been screwed up once, and didn't get
where they were going, come back for another chance. Usually,
they're busted up a little. If not, we make sure they get that way.

This ain't part of a job definition, but this is what happens
when you play football with cardboard boxes. We use the tile
support columns, all around the building, for ricochet shots.
Sometimes they ricochet good, and the box goes in the right
mail bin. Most of the time not. Seems like people working on
the "seconds" belt are pretty much "seconds" themselves.
Nobody cares where anything goes, just passing time. Probably
there's some dedicated workers somewhere but I don't see them.
I was too busy doing what I was doing, mostly stealing things.

Sometimes drugs come through on the belt. Pharmaceutical
companies send samples to doctor offices. I break into the sam-
ple boxes and take anything looks good. Record albums also
come through on this belt. Record club records. I get the bright
idea to print up labels with my name on them, and a friend's

address. When albums come along, I stick my label on it, and send it on its way.

Another guy working on the belt, I get friendly with. Fast Eddie from Brighton Beach, he calls himself. Funny guy. We have a good time together. He does speed drugs with me but that's all. He don't take dope. He sees what I do with the labels and laughs. He says, "you got big balls."

I say, "yeah, and I got lotsa records too." Me and Fast Eddie become friends quick. I tell him about some stereos that me and some other friends got for sale. "Maybe you wanna buy one?" So I bring Fast Eddie to the neighborhood park, let him check out a stereo, and he buys one. Good deal for everybody.

One day, I show up for work at my usual spot on the belt, but the foreman comes over and says, "you gonna work over there today." And he points at a squared off area, made square by empty mail bins. There's a big skid full of mail sacks in the middle. I'm supposed to sort contents of the sacks into the bins. Just me and Fast Eddie. Okay, this may be fun.

Half the time, me and Fast Eddie sleep on dusty old mail sacks. Other half the time we get high in the bathroom, then come out and play with the packages. Then some new stuff comes along, photograph mailers. The kind people send film in to get developed. Each one got five or six dollars inside.

"Nice bonus," I say to Fast Eddie. Then I show up for work another day, and now it's just me in the squared off area. Fast Eddie back on the belt. A lot more boring alone but I entertain myself stealing money from the mailers, and looking for anything else might interest me. Around ten o'clock, I feel a hand on my shoulder.

A big voice says, "you Gregory?"

I say, "that's me."

"Come with me" the big voice man says, while at the same time he shows me a badge and says he's a postal inspector. Uh oh, pig in the mud now, I say to myself. He marches me the full length of the building, up two flights of stairs into an office where a bigger postal inspector is sitting behind a desk.

Big inspector says, "good evenin'."

I say, "nice to meetcha."

He says, "empty your pockets on the desk please."

I say, "why? please."

He says, "'cause I'm a postal inspector."

I say, "oh," and I empty crumpled bills I get from mailers, onto his desk.

Big inspector says, "Is that your money?"

I say, "yup, it come outta my pocket, right?"

He says, "you sure?"

I look close at the money. Hold a bill up to the light. I say, "yessir, that's mine all right."

He says, "then how come these initials are on all the bills?" And he points to little handwritten initials on each bill. Then he says, "those are my initials. I put those there. How'd they get inside your pocket?"

He don't hear this, but I say, "gulp!" Then I say, louder, "beats me."

Then he says to the first inspector, "okay, bring in the skid." And the door opens, and in comes a great big skid, piled high with broken boxes, ripped photo mailers, and some record albums.

"Recognize these?" he says. He tells me, "we've been watching you for a month now. You're a movie star." And he shows me a film of me in action, with stick-em labels, drug company boxes, photo mailers, and more.

I say, "who you get to play the part? It looks just like me."

He says, "not funny, sonny. You're in trouble. This is the federal government, and you're fooling with federal government matters. That's against all kinds of laws. Big laws."

"Double gulp, and holy macaroni!" I say low. "How'd they get all this?"

Big inspector sees me looking like I do, and he says, "I'll tell you a secret, stupid. Up where the wall meets the ceiling there's a thin crack. Doesn't look like much from the outside, down on the floor, but behind the crack is a big hollow walkway. Men watch people work through this crack and take pictures. Like all this star footage of you. Get the picture, flicker?"

I'm thinking, "book 'em Danno, murder one." Something Jack Lord was all the time saying to his sidekick on the tv show Hawaii Five-O. I get some funny treatment now. They do some fast paperwork on me in another office. From an open door in the office I see Fast Eddie talking to another inspector behind another desk. I think, looks like they got Fast Eddie too.

Then they tell me, "Okay, you go home. Show up in the Federal Courthouse tomorrow morning at nine." The reason they don't take me straight to jail is, in order to work in the post office, you gotta get finger-printed right up front. This, plus all they got on me, they figure, I'm not going anywhere, they got me dead. And they right about that. It's my job now to go home and tell the parents what happened. To make matters worse, of course, dad works in the post office! This ain't gonna go over big at all. And it don't.

I down play the part about drugs, and try and make it sound like I'm just a foolish young kid, tempted by candy-like money and stuff, and it's a lesson I'll never forget. Dad and mom so unhappy, I'm wishing my brother and sister were the only children. But they aren't. Dad and mom also had a jerk. Dad goes to the federal court with me in the morning. It's a very quiet subway ride into Manhattan. Dad does everything he can to help. And it helps. I get a Y.O. which means, Youthful Offender. Which means no jail. This was before I got other arrests. This was the beginning of my fame as a criminal.

Judge says, "if you keep your nose clean, and don't get in any more trouble for the next two years, the file gets closed and that's the end of it. It won't show up on your record. But don't make a mistake, son, this is a FEDERAL OFFENSE, and if anything happens in the next two years, you've got a felony conviction in your pocket."

Unfortunately, a lot more does happen in the next two years, including another felony conviction for selling heroin to undercover cops, and four or five misdemeanor convictions, detections, rejections, objections, and what have you. It gets so muddled after a while, I lose track. And, apparently, so do the courts, or maybe I got past the two-year mark, I don't remember. In any case, I don't go to jail for mail theft, which is what the charge was.

Poor mom. Poor dad. They're real good people. They do all the right things, it seems. They took me to little league baseball and everything. They even go to church. Apparently, somewhere, something went wrong.

It took me years later to figure out that good old Fast Eddie was faster than I thought. He was a plant. Just like the photo-mailer money was a plant. He got put on the belt, and in the squared off area with me, just to get cozy with criminal types. To help justice get done. Boy, I'd like to do some justice on Fast Eddie's face all right. But interesting thing, he didn't rat on the stereo deal. Which makes me realize Fast Eddie played both sides of the fence. He weren't such a goodie goodie, like the postal cops think.

Beegee and the Morrise Stereo Caper

Was a factory in the neighborhood called Morrise Electronics. A reliable source of income for local park kids when they were in the soup for money. It got brought to my attention by friend, Beegee. Beegee broke into Morrise's at least a half a dozen times. He always takes stereo consoles. Usually I know better than to pull any caper of any kind with Beegee. He's a fun loving guy but he's got trouble in all his pockets and growing out his ears.

Beegee's kinda funny looking. All the time got a sloppy grin on his puss. Beegee's got a puss. Eyes all about to close, teeth mostly not there. Nose's usually clown red from all the cheap wine he always drinks. He walks with a shuffle so his feet are all worn out in the front. And he wears too big dungarees, and always, always, always got a pint bottle of cheap wine drooping in the back pocket, like a load in a baby diaper.

Beegee's famous for a few things. Been arrested eleven times and still walks the street. Got a brother that absolutely nobody's ever seen. And most famous of all, he was responsible for burning down the Forest Park merry-go-round, horses and all.

Now, I been low on cash, and Antoinette been being held prisoner in her parent's house, so, what the heck? Stereo's nice to have. Maybe we steal two. Sell one, keep one.

So it's Beegee, Big Bell, Feather and me. Feather supplies the car to haul the stereo away. Bell's car got no gas, and nobody chipping in for gas for Bell's car till after we sell a stereo. Bell's job is to yank anything that needs yanking, make a hole big enough to crawl through and lift the stereo out. Me and Beegee gonna do the crawling and hauling. Get stereo up to the hole, then Bell will help lift it out from the outside. He's way too big to fit in the hole. Bigger than the stereo.

All the way there, Big Bell and Feather argue. Bell says Feather's not doing nothing so he should get a small share of profit.

Feather just smiles, says, "you don't want the car, I go home now."

This gets Bell even madder. He says, "you better watch it Feather, I take your car, then hang you onna hook some-wheres."

Feather just struts and laughs, Feather's able to strut sitting down. He says, "not my fault you got two tanks to fill," he shoots arrow eyes at giant belly on Big Bell.

Bell says, "keep it up Feather and I make you hamburger."

These two all the time doing this. Nobody pays attention any more. Bell takes to calling Feather, Zeus, 'cause he acts like King of the Gods. Feather likes the name. And he tells Bell he's the god of thunder, always making big noise.

Beegee leans up from the back seat and says to Feather, "you got any wine of the gods?"

Feather says, "sure, come with me next time I gotta take a leak." Beegee laughs, tilts his head all the way back, sucks long on his bottle of wine. He offers some all around.

"No thanks."

"No thanks."

"No thanks. How you drink that shit anyway?"

We get to Morrise. Us three get out by back of the factory. Feather drives the car a safe distance away. Not really safe, but at least not parked right next to the building. Small window, level with ground, got mesh wire over it, and two bars across it. Bell yanks the bars. Then Bell yanks the wire.

"Good boy, Bell, you my hero," I say.

Beegee says, "this is a piece of cake. I been here so many times, I know it like I know my own bed." I remind Beegee that he's got no bed. He's been sleeping on a park bench lately.

He says, "yeah, that's 'cause my brother Jaygee's home. I ain't caught dead in the same house with that creep." Jaygee the famous invisible brother.

Beegee goes in first. Worms his way in. All of a sudden we hear, "ROWF, ROWF, ROWF. YAP, YAP, SNARL 'N GROWL."

I look at Bell. "Dogs. There's dogs in there!"

Beegee yelling from inside, "BACK, BACK. DOWN BOY, DOWN."

Oh, it sounds like war a plenty. Me and Bell looking at each other like what we gonna do to help. Then Feather starts beeping his horn. "Beep-beep-beep," impatient like.

"Jerk," Bell says. "I kill that Feather. What's he beeping for?"

"'Cause he thinks he's Zeus and can do what he wants, that's why." I pick up a rock and throw it at Feather's car. Feather stops beeping, but he gets out and looks for any scratch where the rock might have hit.

We hear Beegee yelling now, "leggo, those my pants."

Dogs yelling back at Beegee, "Grrrrr . . . rrrrrg."

Bell says to me, "you go down in there and help Beegee." I look at Bell like he just said, c'mon, let's go to confession. But I don't say nothing. No use saying, you go. We both know he don't fit.

Now Feather starts beeping again. He yells from his car, "what you guys doing? playing with youselves?" This turning out terrible. We're making so much noise, and not doing dooty squat, and Beegee's stuck with the dogs. Then Feather pulls up inna car. Says, "whatinna nameachrist you doin?"

Bell says, "dogs down there, eating Beegee."

Feather says, "they're in for unpleasant surprise. Let's get outta here."

This terrible. Then we see car lights coming in the driveway. That does it. In Feather's car we go. Feather hits the gas so hard, pebbles are flying all over. He's going backwards. Backwards all around the building, at some crazy speed. Driving with his arm hung out the window, and his face looking backwards, real casual like. But we're going maybe sixty, and it's pitch black out.

Bell yells at Feather, "slow down, you kill us."

Feather says, "I slow down, cops'll catch us, then you happy?"

Find out, next day, it wasn't cops, it was Tommy LaFrench and Dead-Phily, looking to hit Morrise for a stereo. But they never got to the window 'cause they thought we was the cops.

All that night we're wondering what happened to Beegee. Figure, either cops got him, or dogs ate him. Next day, Bell comes and gets me and we go to the park to hang out and scheme how we gonna get money to get dope. There's Beegee, sleeping on the park bench.

"Beegee, what happen? How you get outta Morrise?"

"Aw, those dogs not so bad, once you get to know 'em. In fact," he says, "lookit over there." Me and Bell looks over at the park house bathrooms. There's a big German Shepherd tied on a rope to the handle of the boys' bathroom door.

Bell says, "that's not . . ?"

Beegee grins, big sloppy grin. He says, "I named him Morrise. He likes wine. Right fella?" he yells over to the dog. Dog just sitting, staring at Beegee. Got a love look in his eyes.

"Beegee, you nuts," says Bell.

I say, "how you gonna feed him?"

Beegee says, "that's why I'm waiting for you guys. I got a great plan."

Bell says, "c'mon, Gregory, I gotta get milk for my mom, she gave me two bucks for gas, you wanna come?

I say, "yup." We get in Bell's car. Beegee's yelling, "no kidding, it's a sure thing."

Bell says, "only sure thing about Beegee is he's gonna be in jail soon." We drive over to a small grocery under old abandoned railroad tracks. This one of the most innocent things we ever do, and it turns into a terrible nightmare. Nightmare on Atlantic Avenue.

Big Bell

Big Bell ain't just big, he's gigantic. He's so big, he's gotta turn sideways going through doors. And sometimes even that don't work, 'cause his sideways is about as big as his frontways. Big Bell's voice sounds like a steam valve on constant let loose, a little muffled. Sounds like he breathes and talks through a mattress. Probably, so much fat weighing down on his vocals, makes it that way. Can't give no regular dimensions on Bell, he's too big for normal comparisons. Best to just say, he takes up two seats on a bus.

His car looks normal except for the driver's seat. His weight got the seat so broke, it touches all the way to the backseat. Which presents a problem when there's more than three of us. Nobody's able to sit behind Bell.

But Bell ain't a sloppy fatso. He keeps clean. And don't smell much. And he dresses the best he can, in big boy's clothes. And he always wears sneakers. Sneakers give Big Bell bounce.

Unusual thing about Big Bell, for all his bigness, he's graceful on a basketball court. And a demon to guard. When Bell pulls up to shoot a basket, all his front sticks out so far, nobody gets near enough to block his shot. And Bell's got a shot. He's got a light, three fingers giveaway that sends the ball on its way, with tiny kisses. The ball almost always goes in. It's sort of a jump shot. Except his feet don't actually leave the ground. Lotta fat goes up, like a mound of jello, then comes down again, and bounces around some more. But his feet stay put. And the ball goes right where it's supposed to go.

Another thing rare about Bell, being so fat and all, he's a dope fiend. Not a lot of dope fiends I know are anywheres near that big. Junkies tend to be skinny, wasted-like. But not Big Bell. Big Bell a prize heifer. But this presents a lotta problems too. No mean feat for Bell to get a needle in him. His fat acts like a bunch of overcoats. Like rhinoceros skin. Tough. Also, nearly impossible to find a vein on Big Bell, they buried so deep.

"I think that's the vein, that the vein, Bell?" I gotta ask.

He says, "yeah, go ahead, hit it." Sometimes me or somebody else gotta do it for Bell, after he works up a desperate sweat missing veins by himself so many times. And once, a needle broke off in Bell's arm. Had to use pliers to tug it out.

But when Bell finally gets dope in him, it looks like peace at last. Looks like a weight lifts off him, and he's burden free. It's almost sad to know fat saddle coming back soon's the dope wears off. Shoot speed drugs with Bell, and it's something else altogether. He turns into a waterfall of sweat, and chews gum like a machine gun, rat-a-tat-tat. But all Bell's rotundness has some advantages too. He's good to stand behind in a delicatessen, or a small grocery store, and shovel all kind of goodies into your shirt and pants' pockets. Can't nobody see ya behind a wall of Big Bell.

But even better than that, Bell aces to go on dope safari with. Dope grows in some nasty neighborhoods. And getting in and getting out of nasty neighborhoods in one piece, with dope, ain't easy. Lotta mugger types, and other plain old junkies, make a living pouncing on people coming in a dope neighborhood. They get you on the way in for your money, or on the way out for your dope. You gotta be fast and dangerous looking and carry weapons . . . or have Big Bell with you. Mugger gotta have a bazooka if they thinking of hitting up Bell. But for every good, there's a rotten bad. Connection never too happy seeing Bell coming. He draws too much attention, and once in the connection house, there's no place for him to stand or sit without crowding up the whole place.

But besides all that, Bell's a good friend. And now we get to the nighmare on Atlantic Avenue. But it only got started on the avenue. It really got rolling in the police station. The day after the stupid Morrise stereo fiasco with stupid Beegee, me and Bell, in his car, we're going to buy milk for his mom. We go to the local grocery store, by the old railroad tracks. We pull up in front of the store. Before we can get out of the car, another car rams up behind us. All four doors pop open, and narcotics cops come pouring out. Seems like fifty of 'em, really only four, but they moving fast. Hands all on us, grab a fistful of shirt collar, and yank us out. Say, "lemme see your license and registration," to Bell.

Bell says, "slow down, take it easy," and he pulls his wallet out from his back pocket.

Cop takes Bell's wallet, then turns his back on us. Then he turns around again, and says, "well, well, what we got here?" And he's got a bag of pot looks like was stuck in Bell's wallet.

Bell yells, "that ain't mine."

Cop says, "well, it ain't mine neither."

Gotta pause here. Worth mentioning something about a particular cop. This Detective Carpetta. Narcotics squad. Story goes, he lost half his brains when he barged through a door on a dope raid, and a girl on the other side of the door whacked him in the head with a machete. True or not, it don't matter. What matters is, something made Carpetta mean. Might as well been a machete.

Carpetta hounds people, and hurts people, and all the time smiles when he does it. He eventually got thrown off the police for holding on to confiscated drugs, and maybe even using 'em. Serves him right. Justice done. Though I doubt he went to jail.

Anyways, Detective Carpetta's gritting his teeth now, saying, "looks like we got us a pothead, ain't that right, fat boy?" And the handcuffs get snapped on Bell before he knows it. Snapped on him with hands behind his back.

And then Bell goes wild. Like an insane bull elephant, he charges at Carpetta, screaming in his steam-valve voice, "you mother fuckers put that there!"

One cop pulls tight in a down motion, on Bell's handcuffs. Another cop grabs Bell by the head, bends him forward. Got a vise grip on Bell's neck. But he looks like a rodeo cowboy trying to hold on to a buckin steer. Bell's outta control. Then Carpetta coup de grace Bell across the back of the knees with a club. Bell goes down like the Hindenberg blimp.

Fourth cop, in the meantime, throws me in a nearby doorway. Slams my head against the wall, and like a magician pulling nickels outta little kids ears, he pulls a plastic baggie full of amphetamines, outta my top shirt pocket.

"Well, well," he says.

"That ain't mine and you know it." I say.

He says, "don't know nothing of the kind." And his knee comes up like a locomotive, into my groin. Cop says to me, "you go peaceful like, or you want to get special treatment, like your friend?" I look out the doorway at Bell. He's helpless, flat on his face on the sidewalk. Hands cuffed behind his back. Carpetta's got his billy club pressed down hard on the back of Bell's neck. Bell's making a squinched face. All red. I don't want no rope and tied treatment, so I go limp.

They take us to the precinct house, in Bell's car no less. Carpetta driving. Another cop in the passenger seat, pointing a gun at us. Me and Bell in the back, handcuffed together. Pretty uncomfortable. Not much room for me. Bell real quiet, except for thick, heavy breathing. Other cops follow real close behind. Carpetta screws around with Bell's car, trying to break things.

In the precinct, they kick us into the cage. The cage is for temporary holding. Real cells are in the back. Cops bring out beer from behind a radiator. Drink a couple of cans. Make creepy comments at us. Do some paperwork. Then my cop comes over, takes me out of the cage, and brings me in the bathroom.

He says, "take a piss."

I say, "I don't gotta."

He says, "yes you do." So I go through the motion. Then he starts asking, "so who do you know?"

I say, "I know lots of people." He kicks me hard inna back, makes me crunch up against the urinal.

Then he says, "you know, this'll go easy on you if you give us some names."

I say, "Frank, Bill, Mary, Bob, Dopey, Grumpy and Sneezy." He grabs me by the hair, bends me over backwards, so his face is on top of mine, and he snarls down on me.

He says, "boy like you can get hurt in a place like this. You tell us who's dealing in the neighborhood, maybe you'll be home for dinner."

I say, "sorry, don't know."

"Okay stupid," he says, and he brings his knee up again, this time into the small of my back. And he brings me back out in the room with the cage. Bell ain't in the cage anymore. He's outside the cage. Handcuffed to the cage. Arms way up high. And his pants is down on his ankles. So's his underwear.

Carpetta's making all kinds of fat ass jokes. And hitting Bell with paper clips. Bell real quiet. Just breathing and sweating. Carpetta looks over at the cops that got me. They do some eye talk. Then Carpetta gets up with a slow, exaggerated sigh, and says, "too bad, maybe fatso here knows somebody?" He takes Bell's hands down, without removing the cuffs, and puts 'em back behind his back again. Bell's pants still down. Carpetta says to Bell, "okay fatso, let's fair it, just you and me." And he takes his badge off and throws it onna desk. I'm thinking, yeah, really fair, Carpetta's got no badge.

"C'mon, you a sissy?" he says to Bell, and gives Bell a hard shove into the outside of the cage. Bell looks so poor. I feel so bad. Bell can hardly keep his balance, with his hands behind his back and his pants acting like a rope on his ankles. If Bell's hands free, he'd squash that crumb, Carpetta, I think. But Bell's hands ain't free.

Carpetta pushes Bell toward a door over on the opposite wall. Then he opens the door, and pushes Bell inside. I see Bell go falling into the dark room. And I hear him land on what mighta been a chair. I only catch a glimpse in the room. Too dark. Carpetta follows Bell in the room, then shuts the door behind him. Then I hear all kinds of noise. Desk screeching noise. Big body, thud like noise. Carpetta teeth gnashing noise. But no sound from Bell.

Poor Bell. Horrible cop. Then I do something stupid. I say to the other cops, "whatsa matter, Carpetta got no dick? That's why he's beatin on us? Got a funny idea of fair fight, whyn't he cut loose Bell's hands, dick brain."

I hardly get the word, brain, out of my mouth, when I get fast shoved down into a chair. Cops put a big thick, yellow pages phone book on my head, then womp the book with billy clubs. They take turns, like men pounding spikes onna railroad gang. This hurt bad. Concussion like. But the phone book makes it so the skin on my head don't break. No police brutality marks that way. Must go to special, creep police school to learn this. That's about it for me. Got nothing more to say. Can't hear too good either.

Carpetta comes back in the room, but no Bell. Carpetta rolling down his sleeves. Got a sweaty hairline. Got sweat rolling down the side his head. He looks at me and says, "whatsa matter, sonny, lose a friend?"

I lost a friend all right. Bell's not the same after this. He's got a permanent rasp-like attitude. What used to be a light bite sarcasm, turns into a rough cutting edge.

I don't see Bell till the court appearance the next day. He looks sick. But no cuts, no blood. Carpetta's good at what he does. Judge's looking at Bell, like, what I'm gonna do with somebody this big? Bell gets a two year probation and release on bail.

Judge looks at me. Then consults the incriminating "yellow sheet" printout of my legal history. Judge says, "well now, looks like you already been a part of our juris prudence system a couple of times before." Then he consults a book, a formula book that tells him, a person does this, they get that. A person does that, they get this. He looks up at me again, says, "by law, you should receive a sentence of one to three years in jail. But considering the nature of the crime, I don't believe society would benefit through your incarceration. I therefore mandate entry into a suitable drug rehabilitation program, to be chosen by the courts, after consultation with the appropriate field experts. Upon completion of the program you will serve the remainder of your sentence in a probationary manner."

Slam! Down comes the judge's hammer. Off I go to Teen Relief, a full time, live-in, drug rehab.

Bell managed to die no more than two years after the Atlantic Avenue nightmare. (It happened while I was away at another drug rehab. Not Teen Relief, another one after that). Story goes, Bell tried to clean up. Got a job on construction. Working on a roof one day, he fell through the roof and broke his heart. I missed the funeral. I miss Big Bell. "G'bye, Big Bell."

Teen Relief

Teen Relief's a place you live in twenty-four hours a day. Sleep in dorm rooms. All boys and men, far as I can remember. And I'm the only white-skin person. Mostly Spanish and blacks.

Every morning, wake up to Jessie Dickson Singers, singing "Oh Happy Day." Really good song, but you get sick of anything if it comes yelling at you every morning from somewhere in the ceiling.

Whole program's focus is on rebirth with Christ. All day, Bible study, chapel service, prayer time, and that sort of thing. Not quite for me, but I see it working for some people, so I give it a try. I pray for typical thing, want God to come in front of me and tell me, "that's right, it's me, God. Now you believe?"

So I say my little prayer, and I kneel on my little knees, and I go looking in closets and under church pews for Mr. Honorable Lord. But no Lord. Least not far as I can tell. But then, maybe this is the kind of thing like dogs hear whistle sounds that people don't hear. The sound is there, we just don't hear it. Maybe august Mr. Lord there all the time, but I don't see?

After a month in the program, I'm allowed visitors. Family comes. Thank you family. Then Antoinette comes. Oh, Antoinette looks so good. She's got a green slinky dress on. Almost a sin, her looking that way in a place like this. We hustle off to a bathroom, and rub and hug some. I go looking for high honorable, august Mr. God under Antoinette's dress. He's not there. But I can't get rid of the feeling that He's somewhere.

I say to Antoinette, "I'm desperate to get high. You get me something?" Antoinette gives me nutshell lecture on getting straight, reminds me why I'm in the drug program. I remind her, I'm in drug program 'cause it's better than jail. I get LSD from Antoinette. Stupid, stupid, stupid.

After the visitors go home, I realize, very sparkle clear, that I'm still here, not going home. And LSD turns my head into rubber. Next thing I remember, lots of Teen Relief people gathered around me, saying, "the devil got in you." I'm thinking, not the devil, just some dumb old LSD.

Next I remember, I'm on a tar roof somewhere in Brooklyn. I'm with two people I don't know, and a midget I also don't know. I think it was a midget, LSD does funny stuff like that. Don't know how I got there. But I recognize what we're shooting in our arms. Old friend, heroin. This feels very correct. This feels like, "ahh, that's what's been missing." After drugs all wore off, don't know what to do, so I go home. This takes some explaining to the family. Why's Gregory boy home again? What I say is this, "all that Lord stuff clogs up the brain, besides, I've been there a month, and now I'm better." Simple logic.

For people who have no experience with drugs or drug rehabilitation, it seems very possible that one month away from home, in a formal drug program, might indeed do the trick. With the help of continued good family support, why not?

This includes the judge and the police. The way the court deal went, if I left, I was supposed to get picked up, and tossed in jail. Those were the conditions. But for reasons I just mentioned, and maybe misguided human compassion, and probably also over crowded jails, the judge says to me, "You did a drug program for a month, your family seems to care about you. You must stay clean and report to your probation officer."

"I most certainly will do that, your honor, sir." I'm thinking this must be where the Lord's been hiding, under the graduation gown. So I try to stay straight, a little. I still shoot dope, but only two or three times a week. Avoid getting a habit that way. And I go to see the probation officer.

Probation

Now, I wanna say right off, not all probation officers are worthless. But mine was. I report to the probation officer in a big office building down around Jay Street in Brooklyn. During the entire interview, the probation officer don't look up at me more'n once.

No, "how do you do?"

No, "how's life treatin ya."

Just, "have a seat." I have a seat. With his head bent down, he goes through form after form, making little marks with a long sharp pencil. He don't look up. He just don't. So, that's that. "Report back to me next week," he says, with his back turned, shoving the forms he just filled out into a grey file cabinet. He don't turn around again till I'm gone. Maybe not even then.

I leave the building, and go straight to the connection's house. I shoot up some dope. Maybe that's what he figured I'd do. Maybe he thinks it's hopeless. Maybe I think it's hopeless too.

Okay, so every week I report to the hear no evil, speak no evil, see no nothing probation officer. And every week he gets my name wrong. And I get so fed up with this, I steal his jumbo size dictionary, and I sell it to buy dope. And he still don't look up at me.

So every week I tell him a different name. And the jerk spends the whole time I'm there looking in the file cabinet for the name I give him. Then he cuts my appointments down to once a month. And he seems more than happy when I call up every other month to tell him I can't make it, 'cause my dog ate my shoes. The game here, I realize, is paperwork. He gotta lay eyes on me every so often, and I gotta lay eyes on him, every so often. And everything else is paperwork headaches.

Dope Weirdo

Got a job working for a loan company. My job is to call people on the phone and harrass them. Seems like a respectable job. Except the place's got maniacs working in it.

The bosses got pervert all over him from his big, grey, greasy hair down to his flubby expensive shirt and pants. Pants look like he's got mashed potatoes in them. Got a pervert grin, looking to do pervert stuff.

His number one collection guy, the guy who goes to people's houses for the money they owe, he's a dope fiend. (And also a pervert). Boss is always hinting to him about sex or drug fun. But this guy's also a genuine wacko. Real crazy. Violent crazy. Probably that's why he's into this work. Sometimes people meet you at their door with a shotgun or two — they ain't interested in paying money back for no money they borrowed. If they coulda done that they wouldn'ta borrowed from the pervert boss in the first place. Anyway, the dope weirdo and me, we figure each other out pretty quick.

"Hey, who you know got good dope?" I say, one day.

"Know somebody over in Long Island City, c'mon, gotta go do a collection there anyways," he says.

"I can't leave the office, gotta make a nuisance of myself on the phone."

"No problem, boss'll let you go with me. Bring him back

some speed and he's happy."

Weirdo tells me, once he put LSD in boss's drink at the Christmas party. Boss goes ducks deluxe in the head and rips the clothes off one of the hot secretaries in the office. Hmm, I'm thinking, do I wanna be associated with these people? I hear boss saying to the dope weirdo, "sure, you boys have a good time, but don't forget about your favorite employer."

So me and the dope weirdo get in the company car. Weirdo driving about two hundred miles an hour on the Long Island Expressway. Got his teeth set tight, and his eyes go from bug wide open to vicious slits. This boy looks absolutely wild.

We get to Long Island City. Dope weirdo says, "do business first."

I say, "okay." Turns out, business to weirdo means dope business. We buy dope from somebody working in another loan company. This is strange, I think, these people in suits and ties.

Then me and the weirdo go up in some strange stairwell, in a dirty factory building. Weirdo says, "this cool." And he starts spreading out dope gimmicks and dope on a grimy window ledge. I'm very worried. Any minute, somebody can come out a door on the landing above us or below us.

While I'm busy worrying, dope weirdo busy jabbing at his arm. He's plunging the needle all over his arm, yelling, "shit, missed again." And he's got one of those nervous twitches. And he's twitching, and stabbing, and digging at himself. Got blood running down his arm in a steady trickle. This ain't good at all, I'm thinking. Wanna get outta here. But don't wanna leave dope. So I stay.

Weirdo turns fierce now. Reminds me of the guy in Psycho, stabbing and stabbing the knife in the shower. Finally, he hits a vein. Gets a little less frantic. Got dope in him. He says, "here," and he hands over the needle. I'm thinking, maybe I go crazy like him if I use the same needle. I don't go crazy, but I get plenty doped. This boy shoot some powerful heroin. Hardly able to negotiate the steps. But the weirdo don't have no trouble. In fact, at each landing, on the way down, he smashes a glass window with his fist. For fun, I guess. We get to the street level. No more windows. Dope weirdo got a completely bloody hand. I don't want to get back in the car with the weirdo. I say, "hey, you go do other business, I gotta make a phone call. Meetcha back here when you done, okay?"

He looks at me eerie like, then says, "okay." I watch him walk out of the lobby, get in the car, pull away from the curb, and aim the car straight at a concrete and steel column holding up the 59th Street bridge. Smash! I don't go back to the office. And I never see dope weirdo again. I go looking for another job a week later. Got to. Probation and family equate job with good social behavior.

Me and Detective Carpetta

Thanksgiving morning, me and mom and dad get a surprise. Detective Carpetta and some of his buddies come banging on the front door. It's maybe six in the morning.

Carpetta starts reading something from a piece of paper. "You're under arrest for sale of heroin to an undercover police officer on the corner of blah, blah, blah one month ago blah, blah."

"You gotta be kidding," I say, "one month ago?"

"That's correct," he says, and he shows me this cheap little index card with my name typed on it. "Here it is," he says, as if the card is proof positive.

"Big deal, I didn't do it," I say to Carpetta. Mom and dad looking confused. What's this all about? They've been thinking I've been straight. Besides, they never knew about no heroin. They just know about "drug involvement" like pot and pills. Not that one drug's all that less worse than another. But heroin? Their Little League, ice cream eater, selling heroin to the police? Dad tries to talk civil, like man to man, with Carpetta. But we already know some about Carpetta. He don't fit the category of man.

I say, "I gotta go to the bathroom."

Carpetta say, "I'll go with you." And he follows me through the house. Other cops in the living room with sleepy, horror-struck, mom and dad. Out in the kitchen I'm trying to make a deal with Carpetta. Mom's got two butterball turkeys ready for cooking. I offer one to Carpetta. Not much of a bribe, I know, but worth a shot.

Carpetta says, "already got one," looking straight at me, and on go the handcuffs again. Behind the back. I don't like these things. I 'specially don't like them when Carpetta puts them on. He purposely clicks them too tight, so the metal cuts into your wrists. And when he pushes you along, like a sheep going for a dip, he tugs on the little link chain holding them together. Makes deeper cuts that way. And if anybody asks what happened, he says, "dumb kid did it to himself, struggling."

On the way out the door, I hear mom saying something about losing faith in all mankind. And dad just sinks in a heap on the couch, was crying, I think. Give dad a hammer, a saw, some other tools, and he fixes anything. But this drug stuff? Poor mom. Poor dad. They got a raw deal here. They do their best, like they were taught.

Outside, the cops got a small station type wagon. I get dragged, pushed and shoved, into it and chained to the floor in the back.

"The floor?" I look at Carpetta.

Carpetta says, "like a cockroach."

And that about sums up how I feel. But we don't go to the police station. We go to Flushing. Cops park the car, all of them get out, except one. They come back, got another cockroach. Kick him in the back and chain him to the floor, with me. And it goes like that all morning. By the time we get to the cop house, they got six of us cockroaches. A mini-roundup.

In the cage we go. Then, one by one, we get called out, for name taking and fingerprint making. Getting fingerprinted is some awkward business. Cop holds your hand and manipulates it like it ain't your hand at all, but some kind of tool instead. Fact that you're attached to the other end just makes things clumsy. And, fact that a cop's holding your hand, showing it what to do, almost fatherly-like, is what makes it extra odd. Reminds me of, "this little piggy." Cop takes one finger at a time and rolls it, side to side, on sticky black ink. Then lifts it and does the same thing on an index card. And you tip sideways when he rolls the thumb all the way to the left and then to the right. Then they give you a paper towel, which you can't do much with but smear the ink all around the rest of your hand.

Then we all get move along little doggied, out of the cop house and into a paddy wagon. These things are miserable. Dark, can't see out. We hit the bumps hard, like riding on a roller skate. And seems like the driver hits every pothole in New York City. We get to the Tombs. Tombs is a notoriously horrible jail in Manhattan. Carpetta's there waiting for us. Out of the wagon, we get separated, us cockroaches. And I get iron-link-chained now to two big men. One's a six-foot-something murderer. The other's a ten-foot, ten-million-pound rapist. I'm in the middle. I'm thinking about those paper placemats you sometimes get in restaurants, the ones that got puzzles on them for kids to figure out. The ones that say, "what does not belong in this picture?" I'm thinking, I do not belong in this picture.

All day long, the three of us get the cattle prod treatment. Pushed down on a bench, pulled up off the bench. Hustled over to the wall. Turn face to the wall. Strip. Bend over. Spread 'em. What they think we got hidden in there, a Tommy gun?

We still got no clothes on. We sit on the bench some more. Stand up some more. I'm getting real cold. And I'm gettin dope sick. Don't want to be chained to no murderer and no rapist no more. Gets so, every time Carpetta shows his face I'm almost glad to see him.

Meanwhile, rapist next to me, keeps bumping me. And everytime he bumps me, I move away quick, and bump the murderer. Then the murderer man jabs me hard with his elbow, saying, "back off."

Then something funny happens. The murderer gives the

111

rapist a fierce look. Like, leave the boy alone or else I murder you. Now I'm thinking, hey, maybe I can get on Mr. Murder's good side with some light conversation.

"Nice day, huh?" I say, looking up at him.

"Ain't been out, don't know."

"How long you been in?"

"Year, ten days, and today."

"How much more you gotta do?" I ask.

"Six years, maybe less, depends on parole."

Seems, these two were brought over from another prison where they been serving their time, for a court appearance, and they're getting processed here, like Velveeta cheese. So why they hook me with them, I wonder. Oh jeez, they gonna send me back with them. Then Carpetta comes along again. He unhooks me, saying to the ten-foot guy while he's doing it, "you ain't soiled my boy here, didja?" He don't say nothing. Murderer says to me, "getcha self straight, boy." He don't look at Carpetta at all. This the nicest thing I hear in a long time. "Yeah, take it easy," I say.

Carpetta got me handcuffed behind the back again. Marching me down some steps. Pulling on the cuff chain all the time. Laughing.

Get down to a cinder block room. Just a table and two chairs, sittin in the middle. My clothes in a heap on the table. Hey old friends, they treat you rough? I say to my clothes, to myself. Clothes give me a weary smile.

Carpetta takes the handcuffs off. Says, "get dressed." I do this in a hurry before he changes his mind. I'm trippin and bumblin with pant legs. Even with clothes on, I still feel cold. It's the dope chill. Need a fix real soon.

Carpetta says, "okay, siddown." We sitting opposite each other, across the table. Carpetta takes his gun out and starts screwing something on the tip of the barrel. Now this ain't no kazoo, I'm thinking, what's he up to?

Then Carpetta sets the gun down, nice and gentle, on the table in front of him. He says to me, "you make it out that door and you're free." Simple as that. I hear the word, free, stand out from the rest. Then I think a little. And I catch on.

"So you shoot me in the back?" I say, "No thanks."

Carpetta says, "what makes you think I'd do that?"

And I say, "'cause that's the kind of guy you are." I say this simple matter of fact.

I feel Carpetta's big foot come under my chair, then me and the whole chair bounce up off the floor. Carpetta gives a glance at the door, then leans over the table at me, all big face and gritty teeth, and says, "I'm taking you apart right here, if you don't go for the door."

Now, I've done some stupid things in my life, but what I do next puts me in the stupid people's hall of fame. I spit at Carpetta. Right smack in his big cop face. It knocks him back for a second, then he turns the whole table over on me. I go spilling out on the floor. And he comes lunging over. Two of us on the floor now, me on my back with my feet on Carpetta's knees, and Carpetta on top with his hands on my throat.

The door burst open, cops come running in, saying, "what's happening?" I yell fast, "crazy loon's gonna kill me."

Carpetta gotta be held back now by the other cops. One of them hustles me out the room. I hear behind me, "take it easy, he's just a punk, you wanna lose your pension?"

I get put in a jail cell now, alone, thank goodness. Cell got a toilet, no seat. A sink with cold water and a dirty faucet. And a cot hung from the wall on chains. No mattress, no blanket. And an old, crumpled *Boy's Life Magazine* on the floor. Hard to tell if it's me or the cell that's so cold.

Time goes by. I get sick and sicker, and more sick. Dope kick makes you feel like you got the Asian, Hong Kong, and Devil Island flu all in a bag. And you in the bag too. And you got a little man inside you, try'n to kick his way outta you and the bag, running up and down your backbone, kicking and pulling as he goes. I picture him looking like Carpetta. All the diarrhea in the world don't get him out. And all the puke and all the sweat don't either. Wanna die.

I ask a guard for something. Tell him I'm sick. He brings me a bologna sandwich on white bread with mayonnaise. And a jelly sandwich, also on white bread. I can't do much with this, so I just sit and wait. And I listen for some familiar sound, something like, "c'mon, Gregory time to get up and go to school." But all I hear's the occasional clicking of the jailer's keys whenever he comes walking by the block. And time don't mean nothing no more. Only thing that exists is dope sickness.

Then I hear jailer say, "okay you, geddup." And he escorts me out the cell, down some stairs, through a hall, and into another cell. This cell has lots of people in it, and outside it. Outside people are all in suits and ties, inside people all come over from Rikers Island for court appearances. Pretty soon, my name gets called.

"Over here, that's me," I say standing up.

Person who calls my name turns out to be a court-appointed lawyer. This boy looks real young. Like just outta college young. He's got a clipboard, and a pencil, and a cheap suit but he looks friendly enough. He asks me questions. I tell him answers. All stuff I've already told somebody else. Then he says, "okay, fix yourself up, you're going before the judge."

Now, this is ridiculous. How I'm gonna fix myself up? I feel like dog shit, and I got ratty, sweaty, mangled-up clothes on. Don't know how many days I been fermenting inside them. Everybody understand how ludicrous this is. Guys in prison pants, sneakers, and too big shirts. And we're all suppose to be looking good for the judge.

In the courtroom I see my family. Got mixed feelings. Happy to see them, but feel so guilty for hurting them, almost wish they weren't there. I'm also thinking, all this for nothing. How they

114

gonna prove I sold dope to some underwater agent? Unless the agent comes visible in the courtroom, and says, "he's the one."

Well, I find out right quick how this little game works. When my name gets called, for the meeting with the judge, I'm scooted through a door, a big heavy door into the courtroom on the other side. This is like Alice through the looking glass. On the left are rows of benches. On the right is the judge. Everybody is looking at me as I come through the door.

The court officer leads me to center stage and goes away. I'm standing facing the judge. Audience behind me. Clipboard lawyer's up by the judge's podium. So's the district attorney. They're all talking to each other. I'm just standing, with my hands resting down by my belly. Feeling so sick. Then the judge motions me forward with a finger. I go up to the big mahogany and oak fortress, mister judge sitting behind. Judge directs my eyes to the yellow sheet's account of previous arrests. Then he says, so only I can hear, "you make us reveal the identity of the undercover police officer, and I'll slam you hard. You plead guilty, and I'll give you drug rehab, with two year's probation. What'll it be?"

I hesitate for a few seconds. Then I ask the judge, "what's slam me mean?"

He says, "seven years up north."

I say, "guess I'll take the rehab. Could it be a room with a view?"

"Take him out," judge says to the court officer.

After a little while back in a cell, I get released on bail. Family waiting out in the hall. Got a week to clean up, before going in the rehab. Seems like I been here before.

As we're leaving the courthouse building, I see Carpetta standing in the lobby, picking his teeth with a matchbook. He don't seem to be looking at me. I'm feeling like big brother had to come help me out of a fight. I'm wishing there was some way me and Carpetta could meet on some fair fight ground or if he got hit by lightning, wouldn't be so bad either.

I Can Do It

Gotta go to another rehabilitation. Another place where everybody lives together, twenty-four, seems like a hundred hours a day. Program ain't a hospital. Don't have facilities for detoxification. You got to kick your habit on your own before you go in.

This program, like most of the other therapeutic communities, which is what they're called, is voluntary. No bars on the windows. No locks on the doors. But if you leave the program, you don't just waltz back in again. And for me, if I leave the program, I go to jail. Simple. Voluntary. Program's supposed to be anywhere's from a year to eighteen months.

I go through orientation. Stay pretty straight the whole time. I got motivation, jail. Shuck off most of my physical habit. Suffer terrible with emotional habit. Intellectual habit telling me a bunch of fairy tale stories about happy ever after, mixed in with Grimm fairy tales of nightmare monsters and what's the use. Spiritual side of me is buried far away deep beyond any listening. Hardly a peep.

This place ain't like the last one I was in. No religion. This place focuses on self-help. Group help. Friend help. No doctors or shrinks, not visible anyway. Usually run by ex-addicts, been around for a while. Been through other programs. Program works, if you ready to make some change happen. We all run the house ourselves. We clean, cook, and do maintenance.

People come in all shapes, sizes, colors and ages.

Boys and girls. Boys sleep on one floor. Girls on another.

I go through program motions. Clean floors, scrub toilets. Go to encounter groups and seminars. But not too committed. Mostly staying outta jail. Till one day I get convinced I can't do this anymore. Too slow. Too uncomfortable. I decide to leave, telling myself, I can make it without program help. Also tell myself, maybe if I get a job, get a place to live, go see stinky probation officer, maybe they don't throw me back in jail. Maybe. Turns out, just like last time, this is exactly what happens. I go see a lawyer. Lawyer talks to the judge. Judge says, "yeah, yeah, yeah, just make sure he doesn't kill anybody." I even get a new probation officer. Old one died of mediocrity or something.

But mom and dad aren't too open arm about this. They're highly skeptical, getting smart to dope fiend tricks. So I go stay with my sister and brother-in-law. Sleep on the couch. Sister and brother-in-law give some good talk and positive environment. I give some good talks too, but the bottom line is, I'm looking for a way to keep everybody happy and still be able to shoot dope, which of course, keeps me happy.

I get a job. Start making some money. Look up Antoinette. She's been in and out of drug programs too. Got cleaned up, like me. But still hungry for dope, like me. Me and Antoinette see other friends. After a while, I move out from my sister and brother-in-law's house and go set up living with Antoinette and a mixed bunch of people. Old drug friends, mostly. What else is there but old friends, old places, old things, when you ain't willing to change into something new? All this time, fairy tale intellectual brain is telling me, "you can do it, you can do it. You got a job, you can do it." But jobs, like everything else in dope world, don't last long.

Job

Got a job working in a place doing pen and ink drawings on pattern paper. Patterns for people to do needlepoint work on pillows. Make frogs, elephants, things like that. I gotta dress up a little. White shirt, nice pants. Punch a clock. I'm doing this and feeling like things ain't going too bad.

I'm living in an apartment, with Antoinette, and Douglas and Annie, and some other people. Faces come and go all the time. I'm still shooting drugs, but only three or so times a week. Keeps the habit under control that way. But this is only one of the illusions junkies keep. Habit's sure to grow. And that's what happens. Before I know it, I'm shooting dope every night after work. And then in the morning, before I go to work. Makes going to work, and riding in on the subway tolerable. And then I'm shootin dope in the bathroom, at work, on my lunch break. Heroin's got that about it. Just like being in love. More you get, more you want. Don't need nothing else, hardly. About this time I'm saying to myself, on ugly subway ride into work, that I'm gonna die like this. Die a dope fiend.

So I'm at work one day, doing my pen and ink drawings with these rapidograph pens. They fill up with India ink, and got a needle-like point for ink to flow out when you press down on them just a little. Needle points come in different sizes. Screw 'em in, screw 'em out. They make fat ink lines, make skinny ink lines.

Coming up on coffee break time. I wanna shoot some dope now. Can't wait till lunch time. I go in the bathroom and start fumbling with gimmicks. Somebody comes in the bathroom, and I jerk up, and drop the glass eyedropper on the floor. It breaks. Oh shit. Shit, shit, shit! Now what I'm gonna do? Got the dope, got the cooker, got the needle. No dropper. I'm thinking and the more I'm thinking, the more I need dope.

Okay, dope fiend gotta do what a dope fiend gotta do. I hurry back to my desk, grab up one of the rapidograph pens, and get back in the bathroom. I unscrew the needle tip, pour out the India ink, rinse it under some water. I cook up the dope. I suck it up in the pen, screw the tip back on. Tie up my arm, and aim for the fattest vein, 'cause the needle tip on the pen is only about a half inch long. And I dig the pen in the vein. Little rubber squeezer, on the inside of the pen, works to push dope in. It works. It's stupid, but it works. Only thing is, it also serves like a tattoo maker. Little bit of India ink left in the pen, leaves permanent black dot. How I don't die from this, I don't know.

Go back to my desk, looking kind of wobbly. People are looking at me, wondering how come I look different. But who cares. Fact is, some people at work do care. They care, 'cause I'm getting sloppy and making little messes on the pattern paper.

The last straw comes when, one day I really make a mess. This time, it's 'cause I somehow lose the baby pacifier. The baby pacifier works as the plunger. On the end of the dropper, opposite end from the needle, you squeeze it and it forces the dope through the needle. I realize I don't have it, after I already got the dope all cooked up. Now what? Well, dope fiend gotta do...

I think, once I get needle in my arm, I can use my mouth to blow the dope down the dropper and into my arm. Seems logical but soon's I stick the needle in the vein, blood comes gushing up the dropper faster than I can get my mouth over the open end. Like I hit oil. Blood just pumping straight up in the air and coming down all on me.

I'm still trying to get my mouth on the dropper but there's blood squirting on my face. I'm a giant, bloody mess, and I lose the dope. I gotta do it all over again. Fortunately, I got another bag of dope. So I do it again. This time, I put my mouth on the dropper first, then push it, and the needle, in my arm, holding it tight with my teeth. This works a little better. Get enough dope in me to calm me down.

Now I do some fast clean up, figuring I'll go back to my desk and nobody'll know anything ever happened. Ridiculous. I got red blood all on my white shirt and probably in my hair too. But I don't care. Got dope in me.

That was the last day at the job. Got nicely told not to come in no more. That's about the way jobs go in the dope world. Dope fiend loses a job faster than a two year old loses a hat and a glove. If you wake up in the morning, and you're sick, and you got no dope, the choice between going to work and going to get dope, tips heavy to dope.

Sometimes, you get to the job, but start getting sick during the day. So you just leave. Got no good explanation to give the next day, so you don't go back. Sometimes, you steal things from the job, to sell, to buy dope. You steal too much, and they fire you. Or you steal from people you work with. Rummage in their coat pockets, or pocketbooks. And that don't last long before you're fired or you get beat up. And besides, no job I know of pays enough money to support dope habit.

Bert and Harvey

Back in the apartment, Douglas tells me, "jobs are for people who don't know how to do nothing else."

I say to Douglas, "whatzit you know how to do, besides shoot dope and read those Russian, Dostoevsky books?"

Douglas smiles and says, "this is it. I'm doing it right now. Right in front of you."

Antoinette peeks a head around from the hallway. She says, "I wanna see what Douglas do."

Douglas is just sitting on the floor, his back against the couch. Got his legs straight out. Bare feet. Got a pile of record albums next to him. Walking two fingers over the tops, looking for something to put on. He looks up at Antoinette, serious-like. And for a second, his head, just his head, looks like it coulda been behind some big desk, doing some big executive desk work.

I say to Antoinette, "don't bother Douglas, he's busy."

Then I say, "got a job interview to go to today. Gotta get nice looking."

"Ho, ho, ho," says Douglas, "you got no more nice left."

Antoinette says, "what time is it?" She's just finished shooting the last of the dope.

I say, "see ya later." And I leave.

On the way to the interview, I'm thinking about how I'm

gonna get dope later on. Got off about an hour ago, and that's only good till afternoon sometime. I get to the place. It's a silk screen printing company. I know how to do silk screen, easy. I get the job.

"When do I start?" I ask.

"Now," says the boss. He's got a blue apron on and a stencil knife behind his ear. He's busy, ain't got time to fool around.

"Uh," I say. And he points me towards a big table in the back. I work till lunch time, then I leave and don't go back.

Back in the apartment, Douglas's still in the same spot. Still fiddling with records. Antoinette's making coffee.

"Who got dope?" I say.

"Who got money," says Douglas.

"I got half a day's pay coming. Not for two weeks though."

"Lotta help."

Antoinette is spilling coffee all over the kitchen. She says, "bet Bert and Harvey want some dope. We can cop for them and they'll give us some."

I say, "Harvey's a pain in the ass. And Bert's such a fag, he makes everything turn to fruit loops around him."

"But Harvey's usually got money. And Bert's funny."

"Yeah he's funny all right. But yeah, you're right. Let's do that." Then I'll ask Douglas if he's coming.

Douglas says, "naw, can't stand those two. Besides, Annie'll be home from work soon. And she gets paid today."

Annie all the time gives money to Douglas. She's the only one living in the apartment that don't shoot dope. She's the only one keeps a normal job. In fact, I think she's the only one that pays any rent. And I know she's the only one with a car.

Annie's very sweet, but so in love with Douglas, she puts up with a high level of madness around her, long as Douglas is somewhere in there.

So me and Antoinette go to Bert and Harvey's house.

"Ring-a-ling, ling," on the doorbell.

Bert comes to the door. "What brings you here," he says with a big smile. Bert's got red hair and plucked eyebrows. And he pounds powder or something, all over his face, try'n cover up his acne.

"You wanna cop some dope?" Antoinette asks him.

Bert says, "sure honeys. Just let me go get Harvey outta bed." And he wrinkles his forehead up and down, where his eyebrows shoulda been.

"We don't have any on us, we gotta go get it," I say, "we need some money up front."

Bert's face goes down like a sad clown. He says, "well, lemme go see what I can do with Harvey. Harvey handles the finances, you know," and now Bert's face looks like a frosted light bulb. He's smiling again, but not too bright. "C'mon in."

Bert makes us follow him all the way in the house, into the bedroom, where Harvey's still under the covers. Bert grabs the covers, playful-like, and yanks them off Harvey, saying, "company here, Harv," and he turns and looks at us for approval. This is embarrassing.

Harvey's not as friendly to see us as Bert was. He grabs at a piece of the covers, trying to pull something over himself. Then Bert pushes Antoinette on the bed. His lightbulb face getting brighter, looking at me for approval again, or something. Antoinette bounces on the bed and laughs. She sees Bert all full of fun, so she tries to increase the mood. This a pain in the ass, I'm thinking. And I'm also thinking, Harvey probably sees this as a pain in the ass too.

Bert says, "Antoinette and Gregory got heroin for us, Harvey."

It sounds more like we got a box of cookies, the way Bert talks.

"Not on us," I say, "we need some money to go cop. But the dope's good, real good," I throw in for some enticement. Harvey wants to go with us. "No," I say, with absolute in my

123

voice, "no chance, connection only deal with us."

Harvey says, "how come you need the money now?"

I say, "'cause this connection only sells quantity, and we're putting together your money, and our money, and a few other people's money." Truth is, me and Antoinette got barely enough to get to the connection and back with no more'n a bag or two.

Harvey wants to know how long it's gonna take and how much we're gonna charge him. He's got a sly grin on his way-too-sober looking face. Harvey's got a permanent sober face. Don't remember ever seeing him laugh. I'm thinking, this would be a lot easier if we just clunk old Harvey on the head.

Situations like this make dope sickness stir up faster than regular. Antoinette sees me getting edgy. So she encourages Bert to get Harvey to loosen up.

"Okay," says Harvey, "but I gotta go get the money. Don't have it here."

Oh, God, I decide right there that Harvey's gonna get ripped off. No way I'm gonna bring dope back to a pain in the ass like this. Harvey seems to pick up on what I'm thinking. It takes forever to get him moving, dressed, and out the house. We gotta walk a couple of blocks to Harvey's mother's house. He goes in alone. Bert ain't allowed to go in with him. Harvey's mom don't like Bert. She thinks Bert's a fag. Harvey comes out about a half hour later with the money. Then he starts in again with, how long? where? when? and blah, blah. Finally, Harvey gives the money over to Antoinette. G'bye, g'bye, g'bye and good riddance.

"Antoinette," I say, "too bad Bert's gonna get burned on this too."

Antoinette says, "yeah, I know, too bad. We gotta make it up to him some time."

"Yeah, maybe we do that."

Now the afternoon's moving fast. "Wish we had a car," says Antoinette, "hurry this up some."

We head for the park, looking for Bell but he ain't around. We swing by his house on the way toward the bus. No Bell car sitting out front. Don't wanna wait no more, so we make a definite line to the bus. Just then, Bell comes toot-tootin up behind us. "Hey, yo, where you two going?"

"We looking for you, wanna cop?"

"Need gas," says Bell. This is a common problem with Bell.

"Okay, we put in the gas, you take us to the connection, we give you one bag."

"Deal," says Bell. Me and Antoinette hop in.

"Take Atlantic out to Palmetto," I say. We get to connection's house on Palmetto Street and find he's just run out. "Who else got something?" I ask.

"Maybe you try Lewis, over on Seneca." We go to Seneca Avenue. Lewis is not in. Banging on the door for a while don't help. Now what? Day going by and we're getting sicker.

"Okay, let's go to Tully, on Bushwick, and if he's out, we can shoot back to Crescent Street. Usually, Mary got something." Turns out, Tully's been busted. His door's all broken in, nobody there. So we drive back to Crescent Street, praying that Mary's got some dope. Gotta call her on the phone first. She got this ridiculous set up. You have to call from one of three phone booths in the area, and you gotta say your name. Gotta be a name she recognizes. Then you gotta ask for shoes. Shoe size means the number of bags you want. This is a pain in the ass.

"Yeah, it's Gregory. You know, Gregory. You got a size ten in a high top?" I ask, feeling silly. Back in the car, I say, "okay, Mary says come on." We drive two blocks to Mary's. I go in.

"Hey, how you doing there my man," says Mary.

"Looking for size ten," I say.

She says, "sorry, all out. Going to get more later tonight."

"But you said . . ."

"Hey, you want something, you come back later."

"Right."

Back in the car I tell Antoinette and Bell how disgusted I'm getting being at the mercy of dope dealers. "We gotta wait till tonight," I tell 'em.

"This sucks," says Bell. Antoinette says she's feeling real sick. Me too. Bell too.

Then Bell says, "I got some Seconals from the vet for my dog on the fourth of July. Noise makes him crazy, and the Seconals knock him out quick. We can crush 'em up and shoot 'em."

Me and Antoinette both say, "ugh." But we both agree it's better than nothing. Back to Bell's house. Around seven now. Bell goes in and comes out with six orange Seconal capsules. Seconal is a strong barbiturate. Don't really fix dope sickness, but it something to do, and it makes you stupid for a while. But they're definitely not for shooting. We try to liquify them but can only make them pasty. This clogs up the needle and most the time, clogs up your arm. Last time I did this, I ended up with fat abscess. My arm blew up like a balloon.

But we're sick. And you gotta do something when sickness comes banging around. So the three of us shoot up the Seconal. We skin pop it, probably blow a vein apart if we did it mainline. And we get real dumb. A little like being real drunk. But we're still sick. Come around nine, we go back to Mary's. Call from the phone booth, "size ten," I say. This time Mary's got it. We cop our ten bags, feeling nothing but rotten by now. Drive to dark, woody area, over by Forest Park. I'm in such a hurry to get lotsa dope in me, I shoot four bags. Next I know, I'm laying on the wet, soggy dirt and Bell's slapping me all over, saying, "c'mon, Gregory, you ain't gonna die on me here."

I look sideways and see Antoinette scratching and rubbing her face, junkie like, saying, "he alive, Bell?"

Now I'm coming to. Trying to make Bell stop slapping me.

He says, "goddamit man, you o.d. you jerk. Lookit you, you're all blue." I look at my arms. Bell's right. I got light blue colored skin. I don't feel too good.

"Where's the dope?" I say.

"You ain't shootin no more," says Bell.

"Yes I am."

Antoinette says, "you do more, and I do more."

"I don't care, just gimme."

Bell says, "you crazy. You die and I leave you here."

"Fine, gimme." Still got three bags left. I pour one and a half in the cooker. I'm cooking it up. Antoinette holds the other bag, and the half bag up in the air, tapping the bottom with the back of her fingernail, seeing how much I left her.

Bell says, "save me a taste."

I say, "sure, we're using Bert and Harvey's dope now anyway. Blue as I am, and groggy as I'm feeling from the overdose, the only thing I know to do is shoot more dope. And for a second, I get a memory flash. Back to earlier, speed drug days. When, no matter that I already took too much, and I'd be gasping for air, and asking people if my head's still where it's supposed to be, or checking in the mirror to see if I still got any head left at all, I'd still be looking to do some more. Looking to catch a feeling that I can't make happen no more. A feeling I used to be able to control. The one I used to get when drugs was new.

How Speed Kills

Got to do a little backwards story telling now. Back to before heroin. Back to when all creativity and life energy, and eventually doom and destruction, came from speed drugs – methedrine and cocaine, mostly. Very powerful. Crystal like. White. We snort it up our noses. Keeps you full of energy, for late night going out, and for overall indestructibility feeling. I have lots of fun. Keeps me chewing gum and happy, ten, sometimes twelve, sometimes more, hours running.

Unfortunately, speed drugs got Jekyll and Hyde characteristics to them. They don't have a control knob for turning them off. And the effect seems to perpetuate itself. Like for instance, I come home after long nights of busy fun with speed drugs and, "hi mom, hi dad, going to bed, g'night." But the speedy stuff don't want to sleep. So I sit on the floor in my closet, make tiny drawings. I pretend to be asleep in the bed so mom and dad don't ask questions.

By five, maybe six in the morning, I drift into something like sleep. But come seven or so, I got to be up for school. So I take more speed, or else the accumulated nasty effect of the chemical wearing off, plus the almost no sleep, not to mention poor diet, all comes down on me like the fall of the Roman Empire. And nobody in their right mind wants that. Snort more methadrine in the morning, makes me bright eyed, bushy tailed, and shiny-apple smart for the teachers.

Of course, this kind of routine got its limitations. I know that. So after a while I figure out to go searching for sleep drugs, down drugs, barbiturates, tranquilizers and such, and I gobble some late in the night somewhere's around before it's time to go home. This helps transport me from speediness to sleepiness. Only trouble is, I get to sleep all right, but sleep don't know when to wake up. Down drug chemicals got me dead to the earth.

The alarm goes off at seven, just like always, and for sure I got to take speed drugs again, to get me chug-a-chug-chug, started. Kick start me into some sort of life movement. Now this is important, since in the world you supposed to keep moving, can't hang around the bed all day. Gotta do something.

But I got a teacher in school who spreads newspapers on the floor in the back of the classroom. Tells me, "you don't bother me, I don't bother you." This works out good since I create an illusion of doing something, and catch up on some sleep at the same time. High school education.

Another problem that comes with working in the speed business has to do with food. Food and speed drugs simply don't mix. Same poles of a magnet. Both of 'em hurry to get away when the other one's around. At home, during family meals, I sneak handfuls of spaghetti in my pockets, and the dog's getting fat under the table.

And another problem is perspiration. Speed drugs make you pulse out sweat all the time, from everywhere. Me anyway. Once, I get the idea that maybe if I shave the hair from under my arms, I won't sweat so much. I get this smart idea from a brain all saturated with chemicals that has nothing else to do but come up with crazy notions mistaken for astute observations. Like, women don't seem to sweat as much as men, and most women shave their armpits and their legs. Methedrine logic is what this is.

So I start shaving all my hair off. Even pubic hair. And I cut myself and I wind up with a red, raw hide, where once there was furry protection. And July and August burn hell into me. 'Specially since I still sweat as much as before, maybe more. But I still got love for speed drugs. With love you make concessions, or just plain go blind to faults in partner, and the speed drug's my partner. Together we keep a steady courtship all aflame. Although it gets like one of them abusive marriages where somebody beats up the other somebody, psychological and physical. And I'm both of the somebodies.

Goes like this for quite some time. I start keeping a journal of sorts. On the journal cover it says, "start speed," and I got a day filled in that's already over a year old. Then under that I got, "stop speed," with a blank space. Every day I look at this and think about filling it in, but I don't.

So how come nobody notices that something's not right with old Gregory boy? He's acting strange, ain't he? Well, some people do notice, real obvious to them, but they're reluctant to speak up. Don't want to accuse. Not their business. Definitely don't want responsibility. Which is what happens, just like if you fish somebody that's drowning out of the water, you don't just fish them out, then leave them on the shore. You got a responsibility now to do more. And most folks don't want to take on that much responsibility. So leave Gregory boy alone. He's smart. No dope. He'll pull out of this. He's just experimenting. Ain't gonna die.

And so I keep snorting up them speed drugs. And the speed chemicals slowly eating away at me. I start getting lots of nose bleeds. And I get an abscess in my gums. Upper lip all swollen out. Go to a dentist and he tells me, "too bad, your teeth are good, but your gums are all shot to hell. What have you been doing anyway?" I don't tell him about the methedrine, but he gives me a look like he knows.

Then my ears begin to plug up. Everybody sounds like

they're talking to me from inside a tunnel. In the morning, when I splash water on my face, and in my mouth, to help with some wake up, I spit out little bits and pieces of tonsil flesh. I look in the mirror and see pits and holes in my throat. And once in a while I cough up some blood. Methedrine and cocaine acting like alka seltzer fizzy inside my skin. Bubble and dissolve.

But you know, all these ailment-like symptoms go away soon as I snort up more speed drugs. Magic. Of course the average person at a time like this is likely to say, hey, this ain't good, and they stop. But this Gregory don't do that. Speed drugs have this terrific ability to seduce stupid brain into thinking that brain is the greatest thing in the universe, and all brain needs, to keep being so wonderful, is to keep having more speed. Unfortunately, old Mr. Nose ain't up to the task anymore. Need to get wonderful white powder in the body but nose route is on detour, under construction, broke down.

Well, simple solution, just need to use an alternative route of administration is all. Speed drugs need access, access happens when you go to a doctor and get a shot, so let's inject drugs like a doctor. No big deal.

Of course a needle and a hypodermic outside the doctor office got that ain't-so-social image. But I get past this since I know people in the neighborhood who do use a needle, for their own personal recreation and medication. Don't carry signs out in front of them, like stay away, monster on board. Maniac. And they're not falling over dead. Just look like regular park people.

One person in particular, named Walter. We call him, Doc. He does this pretty regular, uses a needle. He works for the park department, somehow got a summer job, right here in the local park. Gives out toys, sports equipment and band-aids to kids. And he shoots up drugs in the park house when work slows down some.

Mothers with their children in the park trust Walter

because of the green uniform he wears. Parks Department. With an emblem and his name stitched on a pocket. Long as Walter's in that uniform, he's the man in charge.

In any case, Walter got this job in the park, and he moonlights on the side with his personal drug job. And he knows from needle hypodermics. And I see he's doing fine. Except times when he takes more speed drugs than dope drugs and goes around doing extra work, like tightening up the monkey bars. Speed drugs are like that.

One time I was very speedy from methadrine and cocaine and black beauty pills, and I eyed those same monkey bars. I set to unbolting and disassembling the whole thing. The entire monkey bar maze. All by myself, although, Big Bell, Feather, Frankie and Beegee all sitting on the park bench giving me encouragement, like drunken cheerleaders.

And Charlie Hillman once tried to outdo me while he was on high-voltage speed, by taking apart thirty-five feet of running park benches. Nothing left but the concrete posts. Then me and Big Bell stage a comeback to this while under the vigorous influence, by chopping down a tree next to the park house, and it landed on the roof. Crash! Walter woke up and got mad since he had to explain to the Park Superintendent how he didn't hear no evil, see no evil, and don't have any interest in speaking no evil about who did it.

These are some of the things speed people do for entertainment. Wreck and vandalize parks and things. But mostly they just wreck and vandalize themselves.

So anyway, me, Feather, Frankie and some other people are all at a party. Everybody's familiar with speed. And Doc Walter begins talking about how much better it is, and how much less you need to use, and how easy it is on your nose, when you shoot it. "In fact," he says, "I'm gonna do some up now," and he pulls out his needle and hypodermic set up. "You wanna try?"

Me and Frankie and Feather all interested. We been sitting around the party with tissue up our noses to keep nose drip and blood from leaking out. We all look at each other.

"Yeah."

"Yup."

"Uh, huh." And Feather goes first.

Doc Walter tells Feather, "take yer pants down."

Feather all smiling and embarrassed. "Don't get no funny ideas, Walter," Feather says. Walter grabs two fingers worth of thigh flesh and pinches it, and darts the needle in. No blood, no mess. Skin pop. And Feather starts in with, "oh man, oh wow, what a rush!" So me and Frankie go next. Stand in line for Doc Walter like he's got some kind of clinic operating here.

"What about sterile?" I ask Walter.

"No problem," he says, "see," and he shows us how he burns the needle tip with a match, in between each person. Very hospital-like.

That summer hepatitis moves into the neighborhood. I remember how strange Feather looked with yellow eyes, and his skin turned the color of a bruise.

Me and Frankie we hurry down to the Board of Heath and get some gamma globulin shots. But they tell me, at the Board of Health, that I might be a carrier. Won't show symptoms, just carry it around and give it to other people. Hard to say if this is true or not, although, everybody turning yellow around me, and not me.

Other than going for the gamma globulin shots, this epidemic don't change things much. Scares some people up a little. Slowed down Frankie. Frankie's so skinny and nervous all the time anyway this strenuous speed activity's taking its toll on him.

And Chef-boy-Arty, who ain't using no needles, just snorting speed drugs, tries to tell everybody that a needle is the 'cause of all the fallen angels, and Adolph Hitler, and everything else awful in the world, and if everybody would just play it safe like him, just snort, then everything'll be okay. But Chef-boy only proves that you can go loony tunes from speed chemicals with or without shooting it, after he rips apart his house one day in some mad speed fit.

Far as I'm concerned though, a few little holes in a fat thigh, and some hepatitis scare now and then, feels like a fair enough trade off for relief from all the head, ear, nose and throat suf-fering I been going through. I decide to stick with good pal, speed, and new helper, needle.

So this is like starting on a new job now. Using a needle's got special skills you need to get the hang of. Can't rely on Walter doing it for me all the time. Besides, Walter's got some capitalism in him and he starts charging people for use of his needle, and for his services. Got to pay him with some of your speed drugs. So I got determination to become independent.

But have somebody stick a needle in you is a lot different than you sticking a needle in yourself. First time I try, I remember was in the upstairs bathroom at home. I get seated on the toilet. Got everything I need. I cook up the speed. And I draw it up in a hypodermic I stole from the Board of Health. And after a long time, I finally manage to push the needle into my leg.

But now I sit there, sweating. Can't push in the plunger, yet. Got the syringe thing hanging from my leg. Probably in there for about a half hour before I eventually get the job done. Not easy. Scared.

After that, with practice, clear sailing. No more walking around sniffling, bleeding and coughing up my insides. Plus, shooting drugs is more economical than sniffing drugs. Only need about half as much. Less wasted. Faster acting. But now what happens is so typical of sneaky speed drug. Since I got more left over, I increase number of times I use it. Amazing.

Now I'm getting less and less sleep. Spending more and more time in the closet, pretending to be sleeping for mom and dad downstairs. Fourteen nights in a row once, just sitting in the dark. Sometimes light a candle and do more tiny drawings with black ink pens. Most the time, just sit and stare at the dark. Head taking turns at ninety miles an hour. And I lost twenty-five pounds in no more than three weeks.

"On a diet," is what I tell everybody.

"Gee, he's doing good. What kind of diet is that?" people want to know. But mom and dad say, "you look too skinny, you don't need to diet."

"Yes I do. Lookit how tight these pants are."

"Get looser ones. Stupid pants anyway," dad says.

"Style, dad."

"What's the use," and dad throws up his hands.

Mom says, "pants are nice," she likes all the colors and stripes, "but you need to eat more. Have some meatballs."

Now, with the right ingredients and the right mental personality, and enough other variables in the right place at the right time, a person can find himself, or herself, quick on the road to a very secure position in the business of drug addiction. A lot of evolution and inevitability comes fast into play and in the blink of an eye, you move up a ladder of success, (except the ladder's really pointed upside down). I get a reputation in the neighborhood as a major speed person. Can buy speed drugs from me most any time. Always got some. And always using some. Always.

So much that normal and high got no separation anymore and I go looking for a new way to get high, to capture old feeling when high was new. Since I been using a needle, I only skin pop. Another way, stronger way, is mainline. Mainline is direct. Needle goes straight in a vein and vein carries blood fast to the brain. Quick. Strong. I do this. Evolution. Addiction.

Now, when I shoot up speed, I got to fight not to pass out. Initial jolt is like rocket fuel action. Hold on and hope I make it through blast off, hope for smooth orbit. Gasp, get a breath. Gasp, not to lose connection to brain. Gasp, and hold on, till chemicals settle into some kind of level I can still keep a handle on. Granted, this don't sound like much fun. But the fun comes with the nice smooth orbit effect. After take off. After speed drug got a good grip.

Devil Might Care But I Don't

First time me and Frankie do any dope, we were looking to
bring our heads back to somewhere near the rest of us. We'd
been off in orbit on speed so long. We weren't looking for
heroin. Just some kind of down drug, the usual thing, some barbiturates, a quaalude, something like that.

But chance has it, that old-time neighborhood junkie,
Gilbert, happened to be around the park that particular night,
and he was looking to sell some of his dope (at twice the price
he paid for it). Timing musta been right. Me and Frankie say
okay. And we snort some. Telling ourselves, it don't count, it
ain't junkie-like, 'cause we ain't shooting it.

And I remember how absolutely wonderful was the feeling.
We walk on a fluff cloud. And the fluff cloud takes us over to
friend Cindi's house, where another friend, Sandi, hangs out all
the time. And me and Frankie spend a romantic evening with
the girls, throwing up. I got a wastepaper basket. Frankie's got
a flower pot. First time heroin has that effect on people.

We eventually go home. On the way, talking about how
mellow was the dope. We forget about the throwing up part
pretty easy.

Next day, I'm in a hurry to do it again. But Frankie wants
to put a few days in between. And that's the way it goes. I got
no hesitation. If I like the way it makes me feel, then I want

more. While Frankie, and most reasonable people, got little caution lights going off now and then, and they listen to them. If I got any caution lights going on around me, must be I don't see them. Or maybe I got some psychological disease, like, overdeveloped horseblinders syndrome, or something like that. In any case, the devil might care, but it seems like I don't.

Frankie and Loreene

Frankie and me live next door to each other. We grew up together. Played in the backyard together, went to the beach together. Played sports, hockey and baseball, together. Even joined the Boys Club together.

And then we grow up on drugs and alcohol together too. Start out drinking wine on the corner, on the weekends. Then we took pills and smoked pot. Both of us came to the same realization that pot and pills are a lot better than alcohol hangovers. In the beginning, anyway.

But Frankie's got a fail safe. Frankie draws back on a regular schedule. He don't take drugs seven days a week like me. Frankie's the oddball dope fiend, able to shoot dope, two or three times a week. When the money runs out, or Frankie feels he been doing it too many days in a row, he disappears in his bedroom and watches tv. He avoids cops, and other big trouble that way. And he avoids getting a real dope habit that way too. But he was always staying just on the edge. Just on the edge.

All I can figure is, Frankie's got a fear, and I don't. Or maybe, Frankie's a little smart, and I'm more stupid. Don't much matter either way though with heroin. Whether you're in a fast sinking boat, or a slow sinking boat, the same amount of ocean's gonna cover you.

Frankie's got a girlfriend, Loreene. Loreene's real sweet, but she gets overdosed at the drop of a hat. She don't take a lot of drugs, only with Frankie. Loreene stays with Frankie, but all the time she's overdosing. Gets to be a nuisance. Gotta stop what you're doing and try and bring her out of it. Sometimes she gets so far in the overdose, she starts popping up and down, jerky like, holding on to her's like trying to ride an electric pogo-stick. Takes two of us sometimes. We shoot her up with salt, and pack her in ice, and try to walk her around. Bunch of fun.

Frankie's not much better, as far as how much drugs he can take. When Frankie shoots dope, he shows all the symptoms of the quintessential junkie. And every bit of emotion he's got spills out all over the floor. Together he and Loreene are quite the pair.

Together, they watch tv sports. Mostly baseball. They keep lifetime records on the players. Loreene keeps pencil and notebook track. Frankie got most of it in his head. Not all the picayune statistics, but the essence of the player. Frankie's got a feel for the sport and a heart and soul understanding of the athlete.

Frankie gets real excited when he watches a game. He yells at the umpires and the coaches and the players. He yells loud. Loud, so you hear him out on the street. He stomps up and down, and yells, and runs up to the tv, and shuts it off. Then yells some more. Then puts the tv back on again.

About the time we move from speed drugs to dope drugs, is when Frankie somehow manages to get into the Navy reserves. Gotta go to Navy meetings every so often. Once in a while, for a whole weekend. Usually, for the regular meetings, me and Loreene drive him. But first we shoot dope. And once, Frankie gets all dressed up in his Navy suit, and we shoot some dope, and then he says, "lemme drive."

So Frankie drives, I guess. I guess, because we get there, and only the three of us in the car, and me and Loreene ain't behind the driver's wheel. So, I guess Frankie did the driving. But

Frankie definitely don't know correct driving policies. For one thing, he's got a terrible habit of forgetting that he's the one driving. He's turning, and looking at us, talking the whole time. When Frankie comes to a concrete divider, separating the east-west, or north-south lanes, he just bumps the car over it. Most direct route. And stops the car by running into things.

One time, Frankie stops the car by wading it into the water under the Whitestone Bridge. We're in up to the back doors by the time we realize it. Frankie musta got carried away, what with his Navy suit on. Me and Loreene gotta wait till after Frankie's meeting, when Frankie comes back with other Navy guys, and everybody hauls us out the water and back up the sandy beach.

Frankie usually manages to maintain a degree of innocence. And Loreene maintains the innocence with him. Fact that they stay home alone a lot, makes people think they're okay. So much so, that when Frankie overdoses one time, in the house, his mom gives him artificial respiration, and brings him back to life. And later, she, and everybody else, believes his story. "Not enough greens in the diet," is what he and Loreene got the nerve to say. So his mom makes sure he gets more spinach and broccoli.

This little incident gets Frankie to tighten up his security even more than before. He lays off dope for a while, and fills in the empty spaces with alcohol. And when the heat dies down, he starts in dipping and dabbing again. Me and other neighborhood dope lovers, us caution-to-the-breeze types, we keep moving right along.

And a gap opens up. While we're coming and going in the neighborhood, getting tossed in jail, getting tossed in drug programs, cleaning up, coming back, Frankie and Loreene stay put. Almost frozen in time. And the gap keeps getting bigger. And for the next few years, Frankie and Loreene go mixing alcohol and different down type drugs. Only shooting dope on and off. Turning into relics at the park, 'cause they're so much older.

And Frankie's drinking cans of beer by the dozen. Still keeping up the straight image at home. Drinking beer helps that. Seeing Frankie shoveling snow in the driveway, with a can of beer in his hand, gives people the impression that, since he loves beer so much he must not be interested in drugs.

And more years go by, while everybody else is either locked up in jail, or dead or living in a drug rehabilitation program like me. And during those years of playing safe, Frankie escalates himself into a full blown alcoholic. A beer only, alcoholic.

And Frankie and Loreene get married. And have lotsa cats. And Loreene's taking life more serious. She's got a good job, keeps a nice house, in spite of Frankie, starts developing friends at work, and doing some going out with friends.

But Frankie's going wild with alcohol. Drinking up at least a case of beer a day. And driving his car all over the place. More than once, he finds out he's going the wrong way, nothing but headlights coming at him in his lane, zig zagging all around him.

Pretty soon, Loreene gets good and tired of all this, and she leaves Frankie. Now Frankie's at home alone with the cats and the baseball pennants. But nobody to keep the scorebook. And little by little it starts sinking into Frankie that things ain't worked out too well. And Frankie says to himself, okay, gotta stop. And he goes to A.A. meetings. This works on and off for a while. Then Frankie's dad dies. Then Frankie's mom dies. Then Frankie gets good and sober. Don't know if any connection there, but he's finally sober. Good boy.

Also, Loreene's back. And she's got a lot of spiritual with her. And Frankie, Loreene and the cats, got a house. Frankie told me on the phone. And they busy fixing up the house. And both of them run a marathon recently. Jog. And they watch birds. Still got lots of energy.

Good, Better, Best, Junkie

Living in a crappy apartment now, with Antoinette, and Bert and Harvey and a guy named Red, who broke his nose three times and ain't had it fixed once.

And Veronica McDougal, who, to this day I can't picture any other way than packed and piled with makeup and jewelry. Make up mostly on the eyes, all circled with colors. And jewelry, everywhere. Veronica's got bracelets, rings, necklaces, ankle chains, arm bands, earrings hanging from more earrings, and beads, lots of beads. One time, I manage to see Veronica almost naked, and I notice she's got a tattoo on her ass.

Come to think of it, Veronica very rarely naked. Very rarely shows any skin at all. She's always got lots of clothes on, as if the clothes was jewelry too. And like a cherry on a vanilla sundae, there's almost always a hat plopped on top her head. And one other thing, Veronica's got a monkey. A small one but it shits big on everything. And it tends to hang from over the doorway, and when you walk in, he either shits on you, or jumps on you. Granted, it got its cute side, but more often than not, we can do without a nasty monkey in a crummy apartment.

But Veronica likes the monkey, it don't shit on her. And the monkey likes Veronica, I think because of all her jewelry. And sometimes, we're all so sick and can't move, and the monkey's the only thing shows any sign of life. So we put up with the beast. Like we put up with dope sickness.

So, what's this miscellaneous bunch doing living together in a three room apartment that ain't got much more going for it than keeping the outside, outside? Simple. Dope. We all hungry for heroin. Not much else reason, for me anyways, to be with anybody here. Except Antoinette.

A lotta the time, after we get our dope, or when we don't have any dope, or money to get dope, and not much chance of either happening anytime soon, there's not much else to do so we watch Veronica put purple nailpolish on her toes, or tie some stupid bow in the monkey's tail.

And the way things been going, we ain't capable of much else. Me and Antoinette got our dope habits beefed up pretty thick. And what we been doing for money's got pretty low down. And even with low-down deeds, we still keep losing ground. So we go lower still. Antoinette's gotta sell Antoinette. She says it's not really her, it just happens to be part of her located in between her legs. And the only trouble with that is, Antoinette's gotta go with it. Like a blind chaperone.

Wasn't like Antoinette's in a fancy package walking on the street with it. Not like that. More like, we go to buy dope without any money and Antoinette comes out with the dope. And I don't ask Antoinette a thing. First time I don't even know about it. And from then on, besides checking to see how many bags, and how good's the dope, I stay not knowing about it. And Antoinette doesn't talk about it. But even her doing this, we still coming out on the losing end. It's like the dope monster's got a tapeworm. Keep feeding it but it never gets full. Alla time want more. Roar, growl and grumble for more. Hungry.

And we pretty hungry too. No money to buy food. We make it our business, everybody in the apartment, to steal something to eat and bring it back whenever possible. But Bert and Harvey keep stealing cake and donuts and Veronica steals jewelry and monkey food. And we live with the dope sickness. And we keep sinking lower. So when we walk, we walk stooped over, like real old people sometimes do. Knees about to fold. Getting lower to the floor all the time.

And me and Antoinette been sick so long, never really getting enough dope to wipe out sickness completely, only just enough to keep sickness alive. Shootin up nothing but a thin dope soup. Just keep adding water to the dope cooker. Wring out the tiny, dirty old piece of cotton in it used for a filter, and shoot up nothing. Stick a needle in, watch the blood come up in the dropper, and shoot the blood back in the vein. And so sad after that, 'cause it don't do nothing but make another hole.

And just when it seems like there's no end, no bottom, and sinking low gonna go on forever, is when I find out that some kind of bottommost spot exist inside me. It happens when Red shows up with a friend of his, some creep.

Veronica ain't around. Friend Feather comes by earlier, and the two of them go out in Feather's car. All Veronica's jewelry glows and shines when Feather comes around. She's sick in love with Feather. Which suits Feather just fine. Bert and Harvey laying on a bed in the other room though they ain't really sick, like me and Antoinette.

So, Red and his creep friend says, "c'mon, we gonna go mug some old ladies up in Forest Hills. They got lotsa money up there. Old ladies walk around with a purse full of cash."

I tell Antoinette, "I'll go, you stay here. Maybe stick that monkey in the fridge while Veronica's gone," I add. Antoinette just groans, sitting up on the edge of the bed, holding both arms across her stomach, rocking back and forth like those retarded people do.

And me and Red and the creep go prowling up Forest Hills area. It's dark out. We spot an old lady. Small lady. Got an expensive hairdo, and she's clutching an expensive looking pocketbook.

Red's creep friend picks up a stick. And we start closing in the space between us and the lady. Coming up behind her. And we get right on her and keep walking. We don't do nuthin. And we get a little ways past her and we say to each other, "whatsa matter, why'nt you hit her?"

"What about you?"

"You got the stick."

"Yeah, well, whatsa matter, you some kind of chicken?"

"Not me."

"Okay," I say, "I'm gonna do it," realizing that us arguing ain't getting any dope in my arm.

Gotta find another lady though. We find another lady. And she's got a fat pocketbook. I'm walking towards her, figuring, soon's I get up alongside her, I'll swing around, and knock her on the ground, and grab the pocketbook.

I'm getting closer. Close enough now, I see the lady looks rich. Got one of those rich lady tans. I get one step away from her, and I say, "good evening," and I keep walking. Whatsa matter with me, I'm thinking, hitting my leg with a fist. Then Red and the creep come running up, saying, "you're a sap." Making fun of me.

"Whatsa matter, nice boy, she remind you of your momma?" And it only takes me a second to get the creep down on the ground. I got him in a choke hold so tight, I'm biting my lip so's it's bleeding. I'm choking the creep 'cause I ain't got any dope. And I ain't got any money. And 'cause Antoinette's been screwing some shit-ass dope connection. And all the rotten stuff I ever do, I'm choking the creep for.

And Red's pulling on me all the time, yelling, "get off him, man, he can't breathe." But I keep choking. And the creep's eyes go shut. And his hands fall loose. And they drop to his sides. And only when I don't feel nothing no more, like all I'm choking is an old rag doll, then I let go. Then I let go.

Now Red's trying to turn me around by the shoulder. I shove

him off with my arm. And push him with my hand. "Get off, Red. Go hit some old lady on the head or something. Get off me!" So Red goes and checks to see if his creep friend is alive. He is. But he ain't come to yet. And I don't care if he ever does.

I start walking away, in the direction of the old lady. She's got no idea what's gone on in her wake. I watch her till she's in a lit up area. Till she's near some people. Not near us. And I find out from this that there's some kind of level I can't go to. Yet. But I ain't glad about it. Ain't no asset to a junkie. Junkie's gotta be ruthless to survive.

And I'm walking back to the apartment where Antoinette's sick and I ain't doing anything to help. And where Bert and Harvey's pulling and sucking on each other in the other room. Playing out some kinda, "lookit us, nobody loves us but us, and that's why we need dope." But neither of them got a bad dope habit. Just pretend they do. And where Veronica and Feather are probably high on some dope, 'cause Feather's been alternating, staying straight, working a job, and shooting dope only once in a while. Veronica too. And the monkey. The monkey. Full of life and bounce. But life's too bad to get fun out of watching a monkey.

And I'm thinking about what Dead-Phily said to me on the Atlantic Avenue bus, before he died in Brooklyn in the gutter: "You get through three winters shooting dope, and you're a dope fiend for sure." I wonder what Dead-Phily would have to say about junkie pecking order. Like, good, better, best junkie. And which I fit under.

Junkie Got a Gun

Was about here that Antoinette's parents put out a warrant for her arrest, and she got takin in. The whole thing happened after we burglarized her parent's upstairs tenant's apartment, and the old man living there had a heart attack and died. But they only pressed charges on Antoinette, 'cause that's the only way, they were told, they can force her into a drug rehab. This all got set up by a lawyer her parents hired, and with the judge and the district attorney in cahoots.

In the courtroom, Antoinette got crazier than I ever seen her get. Screaming at the judge, calling him every kind of name there is. Screaming and swinging at her parents, giving them a few of the names she's already given to the judge. And telling the lawyer and the district attorney — who's been trying to calm her down, telling her she needs help and that's what they're there for — that they can all go stick their heads up each other's assholes where they belong.

But the bottom line is, she's gonna get help whether she likes it or not. They got her and they ain't letting go. So, Antoinette first goes to jail for two weeks, part of the plan to make her see they mean business, then into a drug rehabilitation program. Second or third one for Antoinette.

So now, Antoinette's gone. And nobody'll tell me exactly which place she's in, or where. And I lose touch. And I keep shootin dope. I shoot dope till my arm hurts. I shoot dope now like Dead-Phily's told me about. Running up and down my arms and legs. Looking for veins that still work.

Stick and poke iron needles, pop, through the flesh, and break a slim membrane. Break a vein. So the blood comes up in a dropper, where I can see it. Get a good look at the blood. And I got control on the blood. I got a pump. A set of works. Gimmicks. Junkie tools. And I pump the blood. Pump the dope. Pump it.

So now, Antoinette's gone. Outta reach. And Frankie and Loreene's sunk deep in some place and time I can't get to anymore. Dead-Phily's dead. DeWayne's dead. Charlie Torelli got shot dead. Beegee's in jail, again. Chef-boy Arty got himself in a twilight zone.

Then after a big raid on our apartment, while nobody was in, Veronica packs up her monkey and goes to live with some guy. Harvey goes back to live with his mom, which forces Bert to go back to his mom. Me, I go live with my sister and brother-in-law for a while. They got a couple of kids. One's a baby. Sleep on their couch but this don't last long.

One day I'm holding the baby, and talking to my sister, from the top of a long flight of stairs going up to their apartment. I got dope in me. I start to tip over backwards. My sister grabs the baby just in time. I tumble the full length of the stairs. Hit my head on a radiator at the bottom, get up, move out and don't come back.

All I got is a mind made up by dope. Gonna get dope no matter what. I start smashing up locked lockers, up at the school I used to go to. Hustle out all the text books, and sell them to Barnes and Noble bookstore. Then, one locker I bust open got a big bag of pot in it, and bags of dope, and a gun. Now I got a gun.

I hide the gun, sell the pot, shoot up most of the dope, and wake up in a greasy alleyway, in Bushwick. Brooklyn. Got the taste of heroin and vomit in my mouth. And got blood all down my arm. And nothing on me. Money's gone. What dope I thought I didn't shoot's gone too. Musta overdosed. Musta got robbed. Got beat up. Got a lump on my head.

I remember the gun. Stashed it on a roof back by the school. I go to the gun. Then I get back to the neighborhood. Know a bar on Jamaica Avenue with a back window I been eyeing up for a long time. I go scope it out. See how it looks. Don't need the gun for this, except, I'm gonna shoot something if a cop gets a grip on me.

But the window turns out to be more than just a window. Got wood planks across it, from the inside. And they all hooked together with an iron bar, with a padlock on the bar. So I go to a hardware store, cruise up and down the aisles for a while. Then I grab a torch. Not too big. A propane torch. Shove it in my coat and quick, out the door. Man inside the store sees me do this, but what's he gonna do? He's the only one in the store. Can't chase me. So he saw my face, so what?

Around the middle of the night, I get back to the bar. To the window with the wood and the bar lock. Place is closed now. And I set to it with the torch. Idea being to burn a hole around by the lock. And it works. I get inside. And while I'm digging around for cash, I hear crispy noises coming from the back room, where I burn my way in. The wall with the window's on fire. Goddamn torch did the trick, too fine. I gotta get out now through the front door. But the lock don't open without a key. So I bust that too. And the place is orange behind me. Burning.

Not a lot of hours till morning, and I been up a long time. And starting to get dope sick. And feeling bad from whatever kind of beating I took in Bushwick. And the overdose. And the street's near deserted. But I hear the fire engines. Then I see a familiar walk, about three blocks away. Single person, doing a zig-zag, quick walk. It's Gilbert.

I head for him. He don't see me till I'm right up on him.

Then his head jerks up, and I see them stupid kid glasses of his, with the Scotch tape holding them together. I show Gilbert the gun by lifting up my shirt. I tell him about the fire. And for the first time, I turn around and look back where the bar is. Big flames lighting up the otherwise dirty Jamaica Avenue el.

Gilbert smiles, says, "you do that?"

I say, "yeah, by accident. Wasn't worth it either, all I got's about thirty bucks." Then I ask him if he's got any dope.

He says he just shot up his last bag. Then he says, "way hey Gregory boy, you packing a piece, somebody's gonna give us something with that."

I say, "yeah, who you sure got some?" I can't be playing games now, gotta score on a first try. Don't think I can make jerking around from one connection to another.

Gilbert says, "with the help of your friend there, we gonna take some heroin from somebody that owes me." And we head up to the Bronx. Long train ride. I don't say nothing. I got a hand pressed flat on the gun, still stuck in my pants. I think I fell asleep, on and off anyway. One point, in the dark subway tunnel, I catch my reflection in the black window. Even in a silhouette, I look bad.

We get off at Dyckman Street. We get to this three quarter burnt out building. Walk up three flights of stairs, stepping over garbage, chunks of plaster, a drunk. Get to a door. Gilbert knocks and says who it is. The door opens, and we move inside. Feel warm air on me from a kitchen stove, all four burners lit. But inside I'm cold. Sick. And sweating. And tired. Moving from object to object, using them like crutches. I go for a chair. No introductions. And I wait, while Gilbert takes way too long talking bullshit to the woman who opened the door, and a big, great big man, who's sitting at a table, making up bags of dope.

No need for this, I'm thinking, we ain't here to make a deal. But Gilbert keeps talking. He wants to taste the dope. Here. Now. So we do. And that much is a relief. And while I'm untying the belt from my arm, Gilbert reaches over to me and lifts the gun out of my pants. And he yells something. And somebody comes running in from a back room. And Gilbert shoots the gun.

Gun's so loud, everything else stops. Like a sneeze. For a second everything else stops. But the gunshot last longer than a sneeze. Or maybe Gilbert keeps firing it? Don't know. First shot echo, echo, echo. And it's still echoing while I'm out the door and moving down the stairs, whole flights at a time, it seems. And out on the street I keep moving. Don't hear the gun no more. Only thing I know is, the dope was good. Wished I grabbed some on the way out. That was the last I ever seen or heard of Gilbert.

Inside Meredith's Eyes

Hanging on Fourteenth Street and Third Avenue, I meet up with a guy I once knew. Name's Franklin. Not any old buddy or nothing, just another junkie.

And Franklin's got a chick with him. Girl named Meredith. I'd seen her before too. Mostly walking the street, renting out the holes in her body. But once she got put in the same drug rehab as me. Was about a year ago. So I know some about her. I know she's been hooking, to support herself. But also, sometimes she don't hook, like the time she was in the drug rehab. Not shootin dope. Just slow, settling into what she is. She looked fine then. Black, belligerent, and fine. Walked like those West Indian ladies.

"How you doing, Meredith?" Meredith gives me a big smile, and her eyes show so much white. But she's got a clutch hold on Franklin's arm.

Meredith says, "hi, Gregory."

Then Franklin cuts in — "you looking?"

I say, "yeah, I'm looking," and I notice Meredith's face go plain. Franklin starts talking a lotta rich talk. Furs and leathers, and lotsa dope, talk. Says he keeps a lady down on Bond Street, guarding over his wealth.

"C'mon, I'll set you straight," he tells me. And we hop in a taxi cab, which Franklin pays for, and we get down to Bond Street. Place on Bond's a loft, an old factory, turned into a living space. Lotsa room. We get up inside and Franklin lets loose of Meredith, telling her to wait for him in the bedroom. And he calls over the lady he told me about. He don't give me her name, he just tells her to bring out his dope, and a couple of grams of coke. She does it like she's setting a table for dinner. This goes here, and that goes there. And she brings out a nice shiny needle, and what looks like an unused hypodermic. Besides the drugs, all I notice is the lady's got red hair and she's dressed in an oriental-like gown. Silky. But my real eye's on the drugs.

Franklin insist I shoot up some of his dope, and his coke. And I do. And it's good. Then he goes and tells the red-haired lady to do some, while he brings a hypo-full to Meredith, in the bedroom. Then he comes out, and hands over the syringe to the lady. And tells her, "clean it up, then come inside." Then to me he says, "c'mon in my pleasure palace." And he walks back to the bedroom area. I watch the lady with the red hair as she dips the syringe in a glass of water. I get up and follow Franklin.

Feeling Franklin's drugs real hot, I walk through some curtains and now we're all inside the bed, all four. And the lady I don't know's got her clothes off, and my clothes off. And Franklin got his clothes off. Meredith got on white silk underwear, they shine on her black skin.

I keep looking over at Franklin, noticing how big he is and Meredith's busy making him bigger. The girl I don't know's trying to do the same with me, but I don't stop looking at Meredith. At Meredith's eyes.

She looking up at me from behind Franklin's thing. Doing like it's an ice cream cone, and she's teasing me 'cause it taste so good to her. And I'm sinking inside Meredith's eyes. She's pulling me there. And the girl I don't know with the red hair's having sex with me, but I ain't there. I'm inside Meredith's eyes, looking in, not out. And inside Meredith I meet up with junkies I don't know. And some bad looking men, angry men. Men that don't speak, only hit.

154

And they go away and then there's women in there too. Black women and white women, and all different women. And they're telling Meredith, "it's okay, you safe, honey," long as she stay with them. And they're doing things to Meredith that Meredith hardly feels, but she looks peaceful, 'cause it's a safe time. The only time she can drift in her memory.

And I keep looking, not at the girl with the red hair. I'm still looking in Meredith's eyes, and I see her memories. Meredith in a cotton dress, bright colors. And bright baubles tie her hair, tight on both sides her head. She's playing on a seesaw, with little kids. Black and white kids. And she's got little white socks on, folded over once, so a lacey edge almost touches her black, patent leather shoes And Meredith stopping playing, to bend over and fix a buckle on her shoe. Meredith's happy 'cause she looks over and her mama's sitting on a bench with some other mamas. And 'cause she's got a pretty dress on. 'Cause she's clean underneath.

I see Franklin's hands go on Meredith's head. Block my view of her eyes. Now Meredith's just a hooker. A junkie hooker. In a bed with two junkie men, and some lady nobody knows. A lady with red hair.

"You got any coke?" I ask.

"Sure baby, that what you need?" the lady ask me.

"Don't know what I need, but that's what I want. And some dope too. You got that too?"

"Anything you want, child." And the lady I don't know, sounds like one of the women inside Meredith that let her feel nothing.

"Anything I want," I say low.

Franklin says, "what?"

And what I want is to go down inside Meredith's eyes some more and play in the playground with the children. I get off the bed, avoid looking at Franklin, I move over to the table in the part of the loft made into a living room. There's still long, thick lines of coke laid out. Bags of dope sitting in an ashtray that nobody uses for ashes. A nice syringe and a bottle of champagne.

And while I'm sitting at the table, fixing up the dope, the red-haired lady got her head resting on my lap. Her fingers scratching my legs. She's looking up, but her eyes is mirrors.

I shoot the dope. And I shoot the cocaine. Then Franklin and Meredith come out. Franklin says, "nothing but the best."

Meredith takes out a cut-off, plastic straw, and bends her head to sniff up some of the coke. She's got the straw in one side her nose, and a finger over the other. When she tips her head to the coke, her eyes go up at me. And I go inside again.

But not for long. 'Cause I can't find the little girl or the mama on the bench. I only see a paint chip ceiling and a man's face that keeps changing to a woman's face back to a man's face. The only part of Meredith I can find is a small glow, like the last warm coal in an old fire. I don't want to blow it alive. Can't blow it alive. Gonna go out soon.

Dead Man in the Boiler Room

And then I killed a man. I think I did. And I wanna go light a candle in church. I want God to come out and show himself, so I can explain the guy I killed was worthless.

Happened when I was sleeping in a boiler room, in a basement of an apartment building on First Avenue, downtown. Got woke up by these hands pulling on me. Taking my coat. And I'm pulling back on the coat, had it over me like a blanket.

Then I'm up and the two of us are fighting for my coat. And the idea of my coat getting taken by this junkie bum gives me some kind of power surge. And I roll over him like a truck rolls over a dead squirrel in the road. No punches, just power. Force him down and power crunch him.

And an iron pipe nearby crunches him too. Did I do it? Don't remember reaching for the pipe. Don't remember touching the pipe at all. But after the power's gone, there's the junkie bum, with a head all smushed and cracked. And there's the pipe, warm in my hand. Then cold, ice tray in the freezer, cold. Metal stuck to my hand, cold. Hard to pry off my fingers. Feels like the finger and palm flesh is ripping. "But he was trying to steal my coat."

I get out the boiler room, feeling jumpy. Move up First Avenue. Still got two bags of dope in my pocket that Franklin packed me off with. And my dirty set of works, wrapped up in a rubber band, stuck in my sock. Got some loose change too.

I head for a coffee shop, looking for something hot. Hunched over one of those institution thick coffee cups. Every time I go to lift it, I spill some in the saucer. My hand's not too steady. Trying to pour the saucer spill back in the cup, I spill some on the red counter top. Hard, red formica. Waitress don't care. She's used to junkies coming in, spending as much time inside as a cup of coffee'll get them. Waitress got some sort of meter in her head though. Knows how long each junkie's been there. Knows when to say, "can I getcha anything else?" Which means, beat it, you been here too long.

But I got time coming to me yet. Time to think about what just happened. If it really happened or not. Got no pipe burns on my hand. Got no junkie bum hand marks on my coat. Got my coat. Then thinking jumps to what I'm gonna do about getting some money. And dope. For later. And later. And forever.

Think about getting a hold of Douglas. I call from a phone booth in the coffee shop but Douglas' grandmother gets on the phone. She'd be a good match up for Fidel Castro. She tirade and dictate to everybody. She starts yelling at me, "don't call here anymore, don't come here anymore. I'll have you arrested if I ever see you. Leave Douglas alone. He's in a program now. Not interested in your kind anymore." God, Douglas's gone too, I think.

Then granny cracks her heart a little. She tells me, "you know, you might do the same thing, straighten yourself out. The place Douglas is in got a center right here on Atlantic Avenue."

"Thanks, bye," and I hang up. Waste of a dime. And I punch the phone box, hoping maybe some coins will fall out. They don't. Made of concrete, those things. I go back to my coffee. Back to the counter. Coffee's all cold. Milk in it looks scummy. Can't ask for a refill. Letting me be here's all the kickback I'm gonna get.

What I'm gonna do? Already borrowed everything I'm gonna borrow from everybody I ever knew. Lied to them, stole and swindled them too. Had my fingers in every pocketbook and wallet anybody in my family owns. Tried a crowbar on dad's big old office safe, in the basement. Stole and tried to cash mom's unemployment check, 'cause her name starts with an M, and that's my middle initial, but the bank wouldn't go for it. Broke in, when nobody was home, and stole mom's penny jar for when she plays cards with her friends. Jeez.

I push off the counter seat and get on out to Second Avenue. And I nearly bump right into Reva. Last time I seen Reva was on the corner of Eighth Street and Avenue A. She'd been yelling, and chasing me, telling me it was a mistake for me to leave. And she was naked, to prove her point. And, of course, Jerry was there. Jerry already put his hand through a glass window trying to make the same point as Reva. These two had extreme tendencies.

I'd been living and working with them, after leaving another one of them drug rehabs, after getting cleaned up for a while. I was straight when I was with them, only drank alcohol and not a whole lot of that. Didn't fit into Jerry's plans all that much. And Jerry had some very definite plans. Big ones. Prodigious. He had this obsession about perfect. Some kind of Buddhist thing. Every second had to be perfect. If it wasn't he did these extreme things. Like tear down the walls of his apartment. He had an entire building to do this in. He lived on the fifth floor which nobody but perfect people was allowed into. Reva had the second floor, which was also her studio work space. I had the third. More room than I could use. The first and the fourth, Jerry rented out to two old ladies, who hardly ever went out.

The work was design-fashion art. And Reva was the whole staff. A one-person art studio. She did everything. Men's, women's, babys' fashions. All the design work. The illustrations, the type, the layouts, and the camera-ready mechanicals. She did everything, almost. My job was the almost.

My job was to talk to the printers. (Jerry picked the printer.) And to haul Reva's designs up and down Fashion Avenue. I helped Reva with some of the layout and mechanical work if Jerry thought she needed the help. Otherwise, Jerry talked to me. Taught me how to do what I had to do. And told me to read these five books: *The Way Of Life,* according to Laotzu; *Zen Flesh, Zen Bones; Young Torless; The Bhagavad Gita;* and *The Scarlet Letter.*

And Jerry was obsessive about the quality of food we ate. Money didn't matter. We made lots of money. Lots. Jerry had a gift for making money. He knew where and when to do what. Who'd be looking to buy what kind of design (other types of business too, but I didn't know much about that). Reva worked for him day or night. Frantic, but happy, or so it seemed to me.

Other than Jerry keeping a constant couple of thousand dollars in travellers checks in his zippered, jacket pocket, we held the money. A bank account in my name. A bank account in Reva's name. And every so often, Jerry disappeared, and called us from Europe, or somewheres else. And the money was gonna do something, in the way of getting where it was Jerry felt we should go. But I'm still not sure what or where.

But I know what the money was not for. No television, radio, stereo, or any new fangled electronic jazz. Or clothes, only the bare minimum, although, only the best quality. In fact, Jerry's whole wardrobe consisted of two identical jackets, two pairs of pants, two shirts, some other small stuff, and one pair of brown, and one pair of black shoes. At least, that was all I ever saw for the entire eight months I lived with him.

Jerry had a habit of not washing or shaving for days. And, with those same clothes on, good quality or not good quality, he'd start looking pretty bummy, and smelling that way too. But no matter what, he never let up with his mindfulness business. This constant awareness thing. All the time. Got tiresome after a while and I started missing pleasures. Indulgences. My leaving turned into a frantic scene, with Jerry and Reva getting more and more extreme, trying to convince me I was making a mistake.

And the more extreme they got, the more panicked I got. I started dragging everything I owned down the stairs, and out to the street and all the time, Jerry's chasing me up and down the stairs, slamming himself into things, trying to make a point.

And then telling Reva to strip. "That what you want, Gregory? For Reva to fuck you?" Then to Reva, "Reva, take your clothes off."

"I don't want that," I said. "Stop banging your head on the wall!"

I got so desperate to get outta there, I didn't care about my stuff, anymore. But people going by do. They starting to gather and pick out things they like, as if it all was garbage.

And then Jerry starts throwing money in the air. "This what you want? We got too much money. You want me to get rid of it?"

I run around the block, where I got my car parked. By the time I get back, there's a crowd. Partly 'cause Reva's naked, and partly 'cause all my stuff's like a free flea market. Then Jerry got his head in the open passenger window, saying, "you gonna die out there."

I decide nothing's worth staying here another second, so I start to drive away. Leaving everything on the sidewalk, including Reva, who's still naked, waving her arms in the air, saying, "Stay Gregory! Gregory, stay!"

And now Jerry's in the street, in front of my car, saying, "okay, if you gotta go, go over me." I hit the gas. I watch Jerry come flying up on the hood, and roll up and over the windshield, and over the roof I hear him go. But I keep going. Looking in the rear view mirror at Jerry tumbling down the back side of the car, and bouncing in the street. And that was that.

Took the money I still had in the bank account and paid six months rent, up front, for a loft on Twentieth Street, off Avenue of the Americas. And I never heard from, or saw, Jerry or Reva since. Till now. And now, life feels like a sack of shit on me. I got a terrible dope habit again. I mighta just killed some junkie bum in a boiler room and here's Reva.

"Hi, Reva."

"Hi, Gregory."

Reva don't ask no questions. After one look, she starts busying herself in her bag. A big shopping bag. Comes up with a checkbook. And she writes out a check for three hundred dollars. Right there, standing on the sidewalk. Got the bag wedged between her knees while she's doing it. And she says, "take care," and hustles her bag together, and bends into the wind. Gone.

I'm standing there, with the check flapping in the breeze, looking both ways to see if Jerry's somewhere near by. I start thinking how Jerry looks, after he's been unwashed, living and sleeping in the same clothes, for, who knows how long? And I get this horrible picture of the junkie bum in the boiler room. Could that have been Jerry? Now I gotta go back and look. Killing one person two times is too much, 'specially Jerry. If I didn't kill him with my car when I run him over, then that mighta been him I killed in the boiler room. If I killed anybody at all. Sonofabitch, now I gotta go back and look. Besides, if nobody's there, and the whole thing was my imagination, then it'll be a good place to do up these last two bags of dope I got.

So I'm heading now for First Avenue, still got the check Reva give me, in my hand, catching the wind. And somebody pops me on the head. A mild concussion's what they tell me, in the emergency room, in a hospital I didn't ask to go to. But much worse, two detectives are there, saying I'm wanted for probation violation and sale of narcotics to an undercover police officer. Not again? Goddamnit.

In the Courtroom

I get taken to New Queens, a jail hidden somehow inside the
Queens County Courtroom. Nicest jail I been to yet. Newer
than most. It don't have too much crud collected in the corners
and on the walls, yet. And inside got the feeling, the whole thing,
of a tile bathroom. Kinda cool, and hard. And you somehow
know, antiseptic's been there. But it's still a jail. And I'm in it.
Getting processed, again. Fingerprinted, again. Empty the contents of my pockets in a manila envelope. Strip! Bend over.
There they go again. I wonder, if they find anything illegal in
there, who's gonna go get it? But I don't stay here long. They got
it set up so I go in the courtroom, same day. Docket number so
and so. That's me. And here I go, shuffle off to see the judge.

Got medication in me from the hospital, but the dope sickness starting to leak anyways. My head feels fine in comparison.
Got a bandage where the clunk took place. Chains on my feet.

Outside the courtroom my family's waiting. And the lawyer
my brother's dug up is there too. We all stand around in what
feels and looks like a cedar chest. A rectangle-like corridor,
right outside the courtroom, made out of all the same wood
that the courtroom's made out of. Mahogany, walnut, maple,
all inlaid and crisscrossed. Hard and polished. Feels surreal. Or
maybe it's just me. Irrational reality. For sure, I'm the incon-
gruous insertion in this little scene. Nobody else's got chains.

The lawyer's telling me, "cop a plea, cop a plea."

I say, "I don't think I sold no dope to no undercover cop."

But he says, "cop a plea, cop a plea, 'cause they got you now so's they can do whatever they want with you. And this your second felony, on top of mixed misdemeanors."

My family's looking at me like they can't believe this the same boy used to fall asleep on the couch in his pajamas.

In the courtroom, there goes the district attorney, the lawyer and the judge doing the huddle again. All of them are up at the judge's throne, whispering, making a deal. I hear my lawyer pleading my case, mousy-like.

"... Good boy, your honor. Folks are here, your honor. Good folks, your honor. Go easy, your honor. Good boy, your honor."

Then the judge says, "hike," and everybody breaks the huddle, and now it's just me and the judge. He takes his time. Slides a lot of papers around that I can't see, 'cause he's way up high in his judge seat, and I'm down in prisoner purgatory. Then the judge runs off my list of credits. And says, "... for a minimum of seven years and not to exceed fifteen."

"You must be mistaken, your honor, sir. That must not be me you're talking about. I can't do that."

Judge says the list of credits again and points out "you did this, so you get that." Bang. "Court adjourned." And I get duck waddled out the courtroom and back out in the corridor made to sit on a bench. Wait. Me and a cop and some chains on my feet.

Cop ain't saying nothing. Me neither. I'm busy looking for his gun. Figure I'll Butch Cassidy my way out of here. Got nothing to lose now. Then the lawyer comes out of the courtroom, sits next to me. And soon as he starts talking, I realize, it's the game again. 'Cause he's telling me, "maybe the judge will show some mercy, cop a plea, cop a plea." What this means is, I'm supposed to say, Lordie, Lordie, I am guilty. Please, your sir-ship, gimme a chance.

So far, only the lawyer's been begging, and that ain't good enough 'cause he's getting paid to do it. Judge wants to hear it come out of my mouth. The lawyer asks me what do I think? Well, I think I'm willing to crawl on my face if it gets the judge to change his mind about this ridiculous seven to fifteen year sentence. So, back to the courtroom we go. And I'm feeling all terrible. Body all ached, mind pretty dull. Made to sit and wait in the front row, with the cop, and the lawyer, and the chains. Then I get inserted in between some other cases. Standing back up in the prisoner purgatory zone.

"Please, please, please, please, pleeease," I'm saying. And my family's in the background, looking like, please, please, please, some more. And there's this long quiet spell, while the judge shuffles some more papers.

Then the judge says, "if the district attorney and your attorney can show me that a suitable residential drug rehabilitation facility is prepared to accommodate you, and if you, in fact, can make a commitment to me, no not to me, to yourself, that you will remain in such a facility until the professionals who run it say that you have completed their program, successfully, then I will release you in the custody of such a program. But be reminded, young man, should you so much as break one rule of this program or if I am informed in any way of resistence on your part, then you will, YOU WILL, be held responsible for the full extent of the sentence I've imposed on you. If, on the other hand, you do complete the assigned program, and prove yourself fit to live in our society without breaking our laws, then you will serve the balance of the sentence, less the time spent in the program, in a probationary manner." But he warned, "if I ever see you in my courtroom again, you will regret it." Then to the district attorney and my lawyer, "gentlemen, do you have such a place in mind?"

"Yes, your honor, Paragon House," says the district attorney, after looking at my lawyer, as if to say it's all his idea and he's got no choice but to go along with it. "A full time, residential, drug and alcohol free, therapeutic community," he continues, "but there will be a two to three week waiting period, both for orientation purposes, and to allow for bed space. During this time he will attend the facility on a nine to five schedule."

My lawyer jumps in at this point, "your honor, I ask that leniency be considered in setting bail." And my family saves my life again, 'cause they put up the house for collateral for bail. And I'm cut loose.

Paragon House

They say heroin leaves your system in less than seventy-two hours. Don't know about that. Feel like all my vital organs been in a football game, and all my muscle and bone and incidental parts got drug in the dirt. Best I can do is lift a foot here and plop one down there. Bozo the clown I ain't. And today I go in the rehabilitation program. Paragon House.

Don't remember saying good-bye to the family. Don't remember the car ride, or subway ride. Just find myself walking the half block, down 85th Street, from Amsterdam Avenue in the Upper West side of Manhattan. Then up some brownstone steps and pull a handle on a glass door. Inside there's people buzzing around like flies. Run up the stairs. Run down the stairs. Talk, talk, talk. More people talking at the same time than at a tupperware party. I got an umbrella, a pair of gloves, and nothing else but what I'm wearing. A big desk in the middle of the room. A guy behind it acting like some air traffic controller, first day on the job.

"This is me, I'm supposed to be here today."

"Okay, have a seat on that bench," and he points behind him. How long I gotta sit here? I wonder. I don't like to just sit. Especially not on a wood bench. But I sit.

After a while he says to me, "the coordinator'll see you now. Knock on that door."

"Okay," I say. I knock but nothing happens. I look back to the desk man, but he's already busy with five other people all at the same time. Busy. I knock again. Still nothing. So I turn back to the bench, wish I had dope. Then the door opens. A guy sticks his head out, "a breeze blow on the door or what?"

"It's me," I say.

"Who're you?"

"I'm supposed to be here today." Guy goes back in the office, sits down.

Then I hear him say, "come in." So I walk in.

He says, "what's the matter, you don't know how to knock?"

I say, "I knocked."

"I didn't hear a knock." Then to another guy in the office, "Did you hear a knock?"

The other guy says, "maybe I thought I heard a tap, but not a knock."

This office is quiet. Not part of the crazy going on outside. The two guys inside is sitting casual like, in soft chairs. Sit down chairs. Nobody ask me to sit.

"So why are you here?" the coordinator looks all thick, like he's been through some beefy fights.

"I'm supposed to come in the program today." I'm getting annoyed.

The other guy, the assistant director, says, "that's nice, how come?" He's got smart aleck all over him. Got smart dresser on him too. Fancy. Tight fit pants and shirt. Shiny.

I say to him, "'cause I'm supposed to stop shootin dope." And the two of them look at each other like same old, same old.

"That's what you want to do, stop shooting dope?"

"Yeah, that's why I'm here."

"How long have you been shooting dope?"

"Few years."

"Oh yeah? Well I shot dope a few years more than that and

I've never wanted to stop," says the tight fitting assistant director. I got nothing to say to that.

Then the coordinator says, "why don't you cut the crap and tell us what you're really here for."

I say, "the judge sent me. Gotta be here, or else jail."

And they smile. The assistant director gets up with a, "well, I have to be doing this and that and something else. Take care of our friend here."

So the coordinator calls out to the desk man, "get an expeditor down here and have them give this guy a tour of the house."

"Gotcha."

Then he yells out, "and set him up in big Al's room." Somehow, something about this don't sound good. So I go on a tour. Wish it was the Circle Line or something like that. Don't feel like walking up and down stairs. But we walk up and down stairs. Five flights in all.

"And this is over here, and that's over there." I look over here, and I look over there.

"And the girls on the fourth floor, the boys on the third, you got that?" I look at the tour guide like what's he think I'm gonna do, take it upon myself, feeling the way I do, to go sneaking in on all the girls they got? For what?

"We got Black, Spanish, Puerto Rican, Italian, Jewish, Irish, one Indian, and one Chinese."

I say, "I'm Italian," as if like, okay, where do I go?

"Ages is twelve to seventy-two."

"Seventy-two?" I'm thinking it's impossible to shoot dope that long.

"It's about one third female, two thirds male. Mostly junkies. Although we got a couple of garbage heads."

So I'm calculating, population that day, ninety-six. Not counting me. And everybody's busy.

The Service Crew

First mop I get handed I think's for holding me up. Feel so weak, all the time looking for something to lean on. The mop works just fine, long as I gotta be standing up anyway. Got no interest in making no green color linoleum shine though.

Care a lot less about having a toilet bowl sparkle. Only thing toilet patrol does for me is give me a place to sit on the floor and be alone. Forget about any personal toilet use, ain't done that in days. So now I got a mop and a bucket and some little steel wool pads for putting under your foot and rubbing out the scuffs. And I'm swabbing the second floor landing, slow and graceful like. Feel a little like Fred Astair in that movie where he danced with the coat rack. Only I dance with this mop. And I do it in slow motion. Feel so molasses. Like somebody turned some switch and slowed me down. Some . . . body . . . slow . . . ed . . . me . . . down.

They tell me the average time in the program's anywhere from a year to two years. And I'm ticking off minutes till lunch. Swishing a suds mop. Do the little steel wool pad scuffle. Drag a dry mop. Then somebody comes along and walks on it. And I don't care. So what? Then the service crew chief tells me what an asshole I am 'cause my floor ain't clean.

"My floor? I don't want this floor."

"But you got it," is what the chief tells me. "Clean it."

Next time somebody comes tramping on my floor, I took a swing at him with the mop. Hey, it's my floor. But the chief gives me a careful explanation of how I'm supposed to handle this kind of situation. He points to a wood box that's nailed to the wall on the second floor landing, and he tells me it's the slip box. Tells me, "when somebody pisses you off, you don't get violent, instead, you go to the box, take a piece of paper from on top of the box, and write your name and that person's name on it, and drop it in the box."

"C'mon, you gotta be kidding?"

"Ain't no joke," he says, all serious. And this particular guy got some serious. Got some big muscles, and bullet holes in his legs and in his arm. Half Puerto Rican and half Sicilian, and that makes for possible crazy any second. So I figure, if this guy takes this slip box thing serious, then maybe I'm willing to give a listen.

"That's how staff makes up the encounter groups. They make sure people who drop slips on people get in the same group."

"Oh, so that's when you get to mop the somebody on the head for walking on a nice clean floor?"

"No, that's where you tell him how you feel. No violence." And he says this to me like, if there was violence, I'd be dead, and so would a lot of other people around here.

"So then what?"

"So then we discuss where you coming from. And where you going to. Groups is where it's at."

But my experience with the encounter groups is scary, and confusing, and for the first three months in the program—three months—I mostly ride easy as possible. Don't get too involved. Just do a bare minimum. But bare minimum don't go over big. Too many people tug on a shirt sleeve all day and all night. Pester you about, "work the program, work the program." And the fact is, eventually you got to either work the program, or leave the program. Can't slide by, it just don't work that way. Too many dope fiends. Too much desperate. Too much life or death. Even some of the worst dope fiends, people I figure ain't ever been too nice or care about it, even they got the understanding. The understanding that, they don't make this, they'll probably be dead soon.

Nelson and the Barbiturates

Time in the program is expected to be somewhat crazy. Consider what we here for. But sometimes crazier than others. Some people are crazier than crazy. One of them was a very skinny white boy, about twenty years old, name was Nelson. He come in the house all nervous, twitching. Flinch and bounce off the walls.

Nelson stopped shooting dope two weeks before he come in, so folks figure his detoxification was done. But what nobody know was Nelson had also been swallowing barbiturates for a long time. And kicking heroin is one thing, but kicking a barbiturate habit can kill you.

What it did to Nelson is it wrecked his nervous system. Couldn't walk a hallway without his body flinging itself into the wall. Then bounce off to the other side. And when you talk to him, you got to watch out you don't get in the way of one of his arms since they shoot up to his face all the time, twitch, and he smacks himself in the head. The boy dangerous to be near.

Nelson was in the program about a week when one day I see him come walking down the stairs from the third floor, and I notice red lines on his shirt. So I mention it to one of the staff. What the boy went and done was slice his chest up with a razor blade, then nice as you please, put his shirt back on and was

173

going about his business, bleeding his life juice out. Nelson got sent to a hospital and never come back.

Then one day, me and six other people get sent down to the motor vehicle's bureau to take care of some program vehicle registrations, and whadda ya know, there's Nelson, standing in line, or sort of, 'cause he's twitching to the right and bouncing to the left, confusing the hell outta people in line back of him.

"Hey, Nelson, how ya doing?" we say to him. And Nelson goes into a panic, drops all his papers, then while trying to bend over and pick them up, he tips over and lands on his head.

"Holy shit," we all say to each other. And everybody agrees, good thing he ain't in the program.

Ellsworth Johnson, the Third

Another looney person who shouldn't have been in the program was Ellsworth Johnson, the Third. A tall, thin black man. Was in his middle fifties somewhere. Told whoever it was he told to get in, that he already done his cleaning up and was ready this time to stay clean.

"I reco'nizes the need for this type of situation in mah life raht now," is what he was all the time telling everybody. Ellsworth was in the house five days when the little transmission in his head slipped. Was in the middle of the afternoon, in a seminar where we were all talking about values clarification. Ellsworth keeps raising his hand, then standing up and talking in endless run-on, run-on sentences, about nobody knows what.

By the third time he does this, we're all getting groggy and annoyed, partly because Ellsworth's making this seminar thing drag on and everybody wants to get off their seat and out. But Ellsworth just keeps on going. Real slow. Deliberate. Saying, "love in the whorl got to pre-vail, ya knows, an if it take dying to keep on livin, then dyin's what got to be."

"Huh?"

Then the seminar finally grinds itself to a finish and everybody's folding up their chairs and carrying them out of the room, except Ellsworth. Ellsworth just sitting with his legs crossed and he's got a sly grin on his face. Keeps touching the side of his head with one long dried out index finger. Like he's thinking and having great ideas. Mumbling. Pretty soon it gets clear that something more than just being a pompous assjerk is wrong with old man Ellsworth Johnson, the Third.

"Ellsworth, you coming?" And Ellsworth just turns his head, real slow, still with the grin, and now he's pointing the long dry index finger at us, counting. Points at each of us and says, "if a hunnerd has got to die to save the one, then be it so."

"Oh, man, this is getting spooky," I say to friend, Eugene. Eugene just got made responsible for stacking up all the folding chairs, and Ellsworth's sitting on the last one.

"Spooky, schmooky," Eugene says to me. Then to Ellsworth he says, "come on old man, you creased the seat of your pants enough and now you're clogging up my time."

Ellsworth turns to Eugene and says, "and if you must be the first to go, then that I shall do."

Eugene says, "fuck it, let him keep the chair."

Then Ellsworth starts with, "tonight, tonight, whilst everyone sleeps, I will cut the throat of the beast."

"Oh Christ," I say, turning my head away from Ellsworth. Eugene's making swirly finger motions by the side his head.

The rest of that day was spent with small groups of people coming and going, talking to Ellsworth. Then giving up. Then another few try. No dice. By night time, everybody's afraid to go to sleep. We lay awake in bed with things like afro picks and big plastic combs under our pillows, just waiting for Ellsworth to come zombie-like in the door to kill us all, so he can save somebody? Somebody's got to be saved, that's what he said.

Then I hear a lot of scuffling going on out in the hall. And some big heavy footsteps. And I hear Ellsworth's voice, soft and smooth, like palm leaves blowing . . . "this is good, this are fine, we do as must." But the voice is being carried. In fact, entire Ellsworth is being carried. By two large men in white coats. Followed by two more large men in blue coats. And I see them file by my open bedroom door. Ellsworth's in the middle, wrapped up in a white jacket with arms twice as long as his own, tied around him. And just as he goes by, horizontal, his head turns and I see his red and yellow eyes. They got a look, like this is just some temporary side track to the bigger Ellsworth plan.

Then I hear Fernando, in the bunk bed on top of me, say something like, "suyo bombilla esta fundida. Hasta luego, fucking asshole!"

And that was the end of Ellsworth Johnson, the Third. Wasn't the last of the looney tunes I seen in the Paragon House program, but he was the last of the dangerous ones anyway.

Antoinette, Again

Got some seniority now in the program. Got a job as one of the car drivers. Sometimes I got to go to one of the other program houses in the area (they got a number of them scattered around). Usually I just bring some supplies, or pick up some food. Move stuff around. But this one day I get sent over to the 116th Street house, and I walk in, and there's Antoinette. She's sitting with some other residents, sipping coffee. I see her go gulp. I go more than gulp. This is my dope fiend sweetie. My partner in the dope chase. My lover, honey bunch in the gutter girlfriend.

Turns out, somewhere's back when all the dirt and dust was flying, she got arrested for some dope deals and met up with a judge who put her on the railroad to the same rehabilitation program as me, coincidental. Only she went to this 116th Street house. I'm on 85th Street.

So now I'm standing in the main office of the 116th Street house, got a cardboard box of Hawaiian punch, and I'm thinking I must of stepped into some time warp, or this is an LSD flashback. Then a bunch of people realize what's happening and they all start running interference. But I tip up on my toes, look over their shoulders. And Antoinette's twisting her head while somebody's leading her down the hall in a hurry. Next I know I get called into the director's office, and me and the director's having a serious talk.

"I wanna see her."

"You think that's a good idea."

"Yeah, I think it's a great idea."

"Okay, fifteen minutes, in the lounge, not alone. Then you beat it back to your own house and leave her alone."

"Yeah, yeah, sure, where is she?"

He calls an expeditor, and now here comes Antoinette. Big, big smile. Big smile. And I'm smiling. And we smile for fifteen minutes. And we got coffee cups, and they smile too. And after that, after I go back to my house, I'm bugging my director to let me go see her again. But he says, "not a good idea. You two are bad news together. Stay away."

I don't agree with this, at first, and consequently I hear all about how I got a penis in my brain and don't really care about Antoinette for real, only interested in self-satisfaction. Some girls in the program make a special effort to drive this message home to me.

And eventually, I begin to get some understanding of how the program works, and with it, some sense of responsibility, and respect for people who give me advice on what's good and what's not. So I very reluctantly, with a lot of might and faith, let go of Antoinette. Let her go. And as more time passes for me in the program I come to see how I got to work on me, in the present, not on Antoinette, or anybody else, in the past.

Eugene

Eugene, came into the Paragon House two months behind me. His face all pock marks and bruises from old pimples. Got wire rim glasses, the kind John Lennon used to wear. From his neck down matches his long face, tall and skinny. And from the way he's clumsy around things you'd think there was no connection at all from his arm and leg, to his brain. But that was Eugene's claim to fame. He loved to play the fool. Was born on April Fool's day to boot.

Eugene got right into the service crew, saying how, "hey, bro, it's all that's safe for me to do." Eugene was all the time saying, "hey, bro." And he usually punctuated everything with a, "lemme have some," and his hand would come out for a slap. "I can mop the floor, shit, I can mop the floor. You want me to mop the floor? I do that all right, shit, bro. Hey, lemme get some." And he set about knocking over the bucket. Or he'd somehow manage to trip and fall down. Or hit somebody by accident with the back end of his mop.

In the encounter groups, Eugene was more than willing to be yelled at. Which works like a shield, because he's so fast to say, "yeah, that's me, I'm a fool," and so everybody just says, "well, okay, now that we're done with that, who else got a problem?"

Eugene comes from Brooklyn. Everything about him says

that. Got all them melting pot signs. Comes from an Irish family. His dad was an Irish cop. And when his dad's friends used to see Eugene on the street, knowing he was into dope, they beat him up, for his dad's sake. Eugene says it was okay 'cause his dad had respect to keep up, and Eugene all the time was bringing it down.

Late in the program when we were in a poetry class and he starts writing poems, some other Eugene pops out. Now I like this Eugene even more than the other Eugene. But soon I graduate from the program and move into a big loft space down in the SoHo part of New York City with another person I been doing art work with. I go back to college and get real active in positive stuff.

Then I hear about Eugene in jail. And I go visit. First time I'm ever on the good side the window. Eugene is on the bad. Like in confession, some thick glass separates us. Can hardly make out his face. Have to mostly go on voice. And I feel very unusual in here. Didn't like getting searched coming in. I ask Eugene, "how come you in here?" He tells me how he left the program about a month after me, without staff's advice, and went back to his old neighborhood. He got married and he and his wife had a baby. Eugene's very proud of the baby. But he admits his wife ain't no Holy Mary. She shoots dope. And before you know it, Eugene's shootin dope too, again. And both of them get habits real quick, so Eugene hits the street for money.

In the middle of this story I can't help but wish I wasn't there. Wish we weren't in this jail. I don't want to be here, visitor or not. But Eugene sounding so bad, I stay. He continues telling me how he was trying to hold up some guy on Flatbush Avenue, late at night, but the guy turn out to be an off duty cop. Shot Eugene in the arm. And he shot a kid Eugene was with too, in the stomach. They both went to a hospital, then got sent to jail. "And here I am, bro." But no hand comes out for a slap. Can't even see Eugene's hand. Can hardly make out his face.

I leave the jail with a terrible feeling, like dope monster ain't dead, just hiding. And I decide I got to move far away. So I pack up art and poems, take a dog named Alice, and move upstate into the mountains. Big green broccoli mountains, where I figure dope monster don't ever go.

Then I hear from Eugene again. Maybe a year later. Got all cleaned up and wants to come live by me. So he comes up with his wife and a baby and stays at my house, which I rent from two people who only use it in the summer. Figure I'll find another place soon, before winter is over. Eugene decides to try to do the same thing. And we go looking for a house for him and his family. I come across a farmer wants to rent out the little house on the edge of his farm. Nice. They go check the place out. But Eugene's wife complains it ain't got no tub. And Eugene's saying how there's nothing to do around here, and the place's got cows.

"Cows, lookit."

"Yeah, I know, cows. I like 'em."

But instead of moving in, they move back to Brooklyn. Then one April Fool's Day, I'm thinking about Eugene, so I give his folks a call, figure they can put me in touch. I get his dad on the phone.

"Hello. This is Gregory, remember me?"

"Who? Oh, sure, Gregory, Gene's friend. How are you?"

"I'm fine. I was wondering how Eugene's been, and if maybe you got a phone I can reach him at?"

"Oh, jeez, Gregory, I'm sorry, I guess you don't know, Gene's dead!" I say nothing. Absolutely nothing.

"I'm sorry, Gregory, when it happened I didn't think to call you. You can understand, can't you?" I'm holding the heavy black telephone out away from me. Looking at it.

"Gregory, can you hear me?"

"... Yes."

"He started in with the drugs again. And he overdosed."

"... When did it happen?"
"Less than a year ago. I'm sorry."
"I'm sorry too. I'm sorry."

Eugene had a poem. It went like this:
    "Revolution is
    how many times the wheel turns
    as it's rolling over me."

I got a poem too. Goes like this:

"All that's left of my capsized friend is a
    poem and a baby in Brooklyn."

Sad

Now I got sad filling up inside me, close to the top. Start feeling overwhelmed when anything even a little sad happens around me. A leaf falls off a tree, and I stop. Waitress in a local coffee shop brings me french fries, and I feel to cry, she looks so unhappy. News on a radio that a baby panda died in a zoo, and I get terrible inside. Terrible.

I start to call some people on the phone. People I came out of the Paragon House with. People who knew Eugene. And they say, "yeah, I remember Eugene. Too bad." But that's all. They're done. I still got terrible sad pressure.

I take a ride downstate. Visit home. Mom and dad. Family got all this new meaning to me now. They think it's wonderful I got a log house in the mountains. Reminds them of how Santo, dad's dad, came over and made a new life. Rugged. Toughed it out. Funny, after all these years, old fashion comes back in style. We eat lots of lasagna and meatballs.

On the ride back up the mountains it occurs to me that we didn't talk much about Eugene. Or much about sad. And just where a sign on the New York Thruway says, Albany, fifty miles, is where I come up a steep hill, and at the top of the hill I see all the mountains leaning west, toward my house.

I get out of the car face the mountains and yell, "EUGENE!" And the mountains take my Eugene, and send it way far away. Till it's gone. Gone. Feel like I need to grieve. But don't know how. Never had to. Dope took care of that. But now dope's gone. Long gone. And something long buried wants to surface now.

Duras, Marguerite. DURAS BY DURAS
Eberhardt, Isabelle. DEPARTURES: Selected Writings
Eberhardt, Isabelle. THE OBLIVION SEEKERS
Eidus, Janice. VITO LOVES GERALDINE
Fenollosa, Ernest. CHINESE WRITTEN CHARACTER AS A MEDIUM
    FOR POETRY
Ferlinghetti, Lawrence. PICTURES OF THE GONE WORLD
    (Enlarged 1995 edition)
Ferlinghetti, L., ed. ENDS & BEGINNINGS (City Lights Review #6)
Finley, Karen. SHOCK TREATMENT
Ford, Charles Henri. OUT OF THE LABYRINTH: Selected Poems
Franzen, Cola, transl. POEMS OF ARAB ANDALUSIA
García Lorca, Federico. BARBAROUS NIGHTS: Legends & Plays
García Lorca, Federico. ODE TO WALT WHITMAN & OTHER POEMS
García Lorca, Federico. POEM OF THE DEEP SONG
Gil de Biedma, Jaime. LONGING: SELECTED POEMS
Ginsberg, Allen. THE FALL OF AMERICA
Ginsberg, Allen. HOWL & OTHER POEMS
Ginsberg, Allen. KADDISH & OTHER POEMS
Ginsberg, Allen. MIND BREATHS
Ginsberg, Allen. PLANET NEWS
Ginsberg, Allen. PLUTONIAN ODE
Ginsberg, Allen. REALITY SANDWICHES
Goethe, J. W. von. TALES FOR TRANSFORMATION
Harryman, Carla. THERE NEVER WAS A ROSE WITHOUT A THORN
Hayton-Keeva, Sally, ed. VALIANT WOMEN IN WAR AND EXILE
Heider, Ulrike. ANARCHISM: Left Right & Green
Herron, Don. THE DASHIELL HAMMETT TOUR: A Guidebook
Herron, Don. THE LITERARY WORLD OF SAN FRANCISCO
Higman, Perry, tr. LOVE POEMS FROM SPAIN AND SPANISH AMERICA
Jaffe, Harold. EROS: ANTI-EROS
Jenkins, Edith. AGAINST A FIELD SINISTER
Katzenberger, Elaine, ed. FIRST WORLD, HA HA HA!
Kerouac, Jack. BOOK OF DREAMS
Kerouac, Jack. POMES ALL SIZES
Kerouac, Jack. SCATTERED POEMS
Kerouac, Jack. SCRIPTURE OF THE GOLDEN ETERNITY
Lacarrière, Jacques. THE GNOSTICS
La Duke, Betty. COMPAÑERAS
La Loca. ADVENTURES ON THE ISLE OF ADOLESCENCE
Lamantia, Philip. MEADOWLARK WEST
Laughlin, James. SELECTED POEMS: 1935–1985
Le Brun, Annie. SADE: On the Brink of the Abyss
Lowry, Malcolm. SELECTED POEMS
Mackey, Nathaniel. SCHOOL OF UDHRA
Marcelin, Philippe-Thoby. THE BEAST OF THE HAITIAN HILLS
Masereel, Frans. PASSIONATE JOURNEY
Mayakovsky, Vladimir. LISTEN! EARLY POEMS
Mrabet, Mohammed. THE BOY WHO SET THE FIRE

Mrabet, Mohammed. THE LEMON
Mrabet, Mohammed. LOVE WITH A FEW HAIRS
Mrabet, Mohammed. M'HASHISH
Murguía, A. & B. Paschke, eds. VOLCAN: Poems from Central America
Murillo, Rosario. ANGEL IN THE DELUGE
Parenti, Michael. AGAINST EMPIRE
Paschke, B. & D. Volpendesta, eds. CLAMOR OF INNOCENCE
Pasolini, Pier Paolo. ROMAN POEMS
Pessoa, Fernando. ALWAYS ASTONISHED
Peters, Nancy J., ed. WAR AFTER WAR (City Lights Review #5)
Poe, Edgar Allan. THE UNKNOWN POE
Porta, Antonio. KISSES FROM ANOTHER DREAM
Prévert, Jacques. PAROLES
Purdy, James. THE CANDLES OF YOUR EYES
Purdy, James. GARMENTS THE LIVING WEAR
Purdy, James. IN A SHALLOW GRAVE
Purdy, James. OUT WITH THE STARS
Rachlin, Nahid. MARRIED TO A STRANGER
Rachlin, Nahid. VEILS: SHORT STORIES
Reed, Jeremy. DELIRIUM: An Interpretation of Arthur Rimbaud
Reed, Jeremy. RED-HAIRED ANDROID
Rey Rosa, Rodrigo. THE BEGGAR'S KNIFE
Rey Rosa, Rodrigo. DUST ON HER TONGUE
Rigaud, Milo. SECRETS OF VOODOO
Ruy Sánchez, Alberto. MOGADOR
Saadawi, Nawal El. MEMOIRS OF A WOMAN DOCTOR
Sawyer-Lauçanno, Christopher, transl. THE DESTRUCTION OF
    THE JAGUAR
Scholder, Amy, ed. CRITICAL CONDITION: Women on the Edge
    of Violence
Sclauzero, Mariarosa. MARLENE
Serge, Victor. RESISTANCE
Shepard, Sam. MOTEL CHRONICLES
Shepard, Sam. FOOL FOR LOVE & THE SAD LAMENT OF PECOS BILL
Smith, Michael. IT A COME
Snyder, Gary. THE OLD WAYS
Solnit, Rebecca. SECRET EXHIBITION: Six California Artists
Sussler, Betsy, ed. BOMB: INTERVIEWS
Takahashi, Mutsuo. SLEEPING SINNING FALLING
Turyn, Anne, ed. TOP TOP STORIES
Tutuola, Amos. FEATHER WOMAN OF THE JUNGLE
Tutuola, Amos. SIMBI & THE SATYR OF THE DARK JUNGLE
Valaoritis, Nanos. MY AFTERLIFE GUARANTEED
Veltri, George. NICE BOY
Wilson, Colin. POETRY AND MYSTICISM
Wilson, Peter Lamborn. SACRED DRIFT
Wynne, John. THE OTHER WORLD
Zamora, Daisy. RIVERBED OF MEMORY